# THE SPIRIT OF *Christmas*
## STORIES OF THE SEASON

# THE SPIRIT OF Christmas
## STORIES OF THE SEASON

FICTIONAL CHRISTMAS STORIES BY
BELOVED LDS AUTHORS

JENNIE HANSEN,
BETSY BRANNON GREEN,
AND MICHELE ASHMAN BELL

Covenant Communications, Inc.

Cover image: *Red Christmas Ornament* by Fancy Photography © Veer.com.
Cover design copyrighted 2008 by Covenant Communications, Inc.

Published by Covenant Communications, Inc.
American Fork, Utah

Copyright © 2008 by Jennie Hansen, Betsy Brannon Green, and Michele Ashman Bell

All rights reserved. No part of this book may be reproduced in any format or in any medium without the written permission of the publisher, Covenant Communications, Inc., P.O. Box 416, American Fork, UT 84003. The views expressed within this work are the sole responsibility of the author and do not necessarily reflect the position of Covenant Communications, Inc., or any other entity.

This is a work of fiction. The characters, names, incidents, places, and dialogue are products of the authors' imagination, and are not to be construed as real.

Printed in Canada
First Printing: October 2008

14 13 12 11 10 09 08      10 9 8 7 6 5 4 3 2 1

ISBN 13: 978-1-59811-581-9
ISBN 10: 1-59811-581-2

# The Best Christmas Ever
## by Jennie Hansen

At the conclusion of World War II, life was still hard in small rural towns and farms, but there was an air of optimism and hope as those communities returned to the traditions set aside during the war years. Arco, Idaho, had a new fire truck, and the announcement had gone out on the radio that Santa would arrive on the back of that truck on Saturday. Janie had heard the announcement, and it had become her fondest wish that she be present to welcome him.

"I want to go. Please take me," Janie pleaded.

"I don't know. It's awfully cold." Daddy looked like he might be considering her request. "You better ask Mama."

"Oh, please, Mama. I want to see Santa Claus." Janie hopped on one foot for emphasis.

"Daddy's going to be too busy to watch you, and you're awfully young." Mama patted the baby's back and resumed feeding him.

"I'm five now, and Margie gets to go. Daddy said I had to ask you." Janie used her best coaxing voice. It wasn't fair; she was always too young to do the fun things her older brothers and sister did, but she wasn't a baby like the twins and little David. She'd turned five just last month.

"Margie is seven. That's much older than four."

"Five."

"I don't know . . ." Mama's voice trailed off and she looked at Daddy over Janie's head. After a moment, she turned back to Janie. "If you promise to be really good, I'll let you go. But you have to dress warmly. That means the snow pants cousin Darrell gave you and—"

"They're boy pants."

"You'll wear them or you won't go."

"All right." She dragged out the words. If wearing her cousin's hand-me-down snow pants was the only way she could see Santa Claus, she'd wear the pants. She ran to fetch them from the nail on the back porch where they'd hung for almost a month, ever since Aunt Edith had brought a box of clothes her boys had outgrown.

Sitting on the floor, Janie pulled off her shoes and began tugging at the ugly brown pants. She had them almost to her waist and was tucking her dress inside them when Margie asked why she was putting on the detested pants.

"I'm going to see Santa Claus. This will be the very best Christmas."

"Do I have to watch Janie?" Margie turned to their mother, disappointment clear in her voice.

A little ache started in Janie's heart. Margie didn't seem happy that Janie was going to see Santa Claus. Sometimes she wondered if her family liked her even a little bit. It seemed no one wanted to include her when they did something fun.

"She promised to mind," Mama said. "Daddy and the boys will all help too."

"They won't," Margie grumbled under her breath, making Janie feel sad again for just a moment before she remembered she was going to see Santa and ran to fetch her boots.

"Are *they* going?" all three of Janie's older brothers asked when they saw Janie and Margie dressed in their heavy winter clothes.

"Sure." Daddy clapped his gloved hands together. "Santa only comes once a year, and they want to see him. They won't be any trouble for us four men to look after."

"We've got our shopping to do. We can't do that if our little sisters are watching," Ralph complained.

"I'm meeting some of the guys," Jerry protested.

"I'm not going to be stuck tending the girls by myself." Ron glared at his brothers.

"Shhh, you'll wake the twins, and they'll want to go." Mama placed a finger to her lips, but her words were warning enough. The boys immediately softened their voices. The whole family had learned it wasn't wise to wake the two-year-olds from their naps prematurely.

"We'll work something out." Daddy made a shooing motion with his hands, ushering the children out the door. He gave Mama a peck on the cheek before following them. Moments later, the boys were piled in the backseat of the Willy, while Janie sat next to Margie in the front.

Janie pressed her face against the car window and peered through the circle her breath created on the frosty glass. There was nothing to see but a monotonous bank of snow that seemed to stretch endlessly alongside the road. Daddy had remarked several times to Mama that there had been a record snowfall this year and that he didn't remember another year when so much snow and low temperatures had arrived so early.

The trip to town always seemed long, but this day it seemed to go on forever. Santa Claus was going to be in town, and Janie didn't want to miss him. She couldn't help squirming as she squinted through the windshield.

"When Santa Claus comes, he always gives each kid a sack of treats," Margie explained in her superior big-sister voice. Her eyes danced with merriment as she shared the good news. Janie suspected Margie was as excited as she was.

"What kind of treats?" Janie asked, though she already knew the answer. Their older brothers remembered the peanuts and candy from before the war. They'd shared that item of news when they heard the radio announcer's exciting news.

"Mostly there will be peanuts, but at the very bottom of the paper bag will be hard candy," Margie said with undisguised excitement in her voice.

"And a chocolate," Janie prompted. Mama had shared that exciting tidbit of news.

"Yes, a chocolate. And an orange." The last part came out as almost a sigh.

"An orange?" That was the best part. Oranges were a rare treat in the family's Idaho farm home. They were reserved for the toes of Christmas stockings, and occasionally Mama would buy a small bag of them when her hens had been particularly productive and she had a few extra coins to buy the children a treat. She would peel the golden fruit quickly with her fingers, then give each of the children a section, just enough to leave them longing for more.

*The Spirit of Christmas: Stories of the Season*

"Will Santa Claus give me a whole orange for myself?" Janie asked.

"Nah! He'll give you a lump of coal," Ralph said. Her other two older brothers joined in, warning that coal would be in her sack. "Naughty kids just get coal for Christmas."

"I'm not naughty," she said, but the accusation left an uncomfortable worry in her heart.

"Remember when you left the chicken coop door unlatched?"

"And fed your oatmeal to the pigs?"

"Then there's the matter of taking the twins swimming in the ditch."

"And riding the new colt."

"That's enough," Daddy cautioned in a stern voice.

Janie turned to Margie, worried.

"He won't give you coal," Margie assured her, and Janie snuggled closer to her big sister. "Even if you deserve it."

Margie was almost three years older than Janie, but in their large, busy household she'd taken on the role of "little mother" to Janie and was often charged with looking after her. Janie knew she tried her sister's patience, but they were best friends too. It was just that Margie always wanted to play house or take their dolls for buggy rides while Janie preferred climbing trees and catching frogs.

"I don't think Santa is going to make it this year," Ron stated solemnly from the backseat. "I heard his reindeer got stuck in a snowdrift."

"If he has to walk, he'll never make it," Jerry added. "He's too old and fat to walk all the way to town. We might as well turn around and go back home."

Tears pricked the back of Janie's eyes. She couldn't bear to give up on seeing Santa Claus.

"They're teasing," Margie whispered. "Santa doesn't bring his sleigh when he visits town. His sleigh and reindeer are only magical on Christmas Eve. Remember, he's coming on the new fire truck."

Janie felt somewhat comforted but wondered why none of Mama's books mentioned that Santa Claus sometimes arrived on a fire truck. Every picture in her books showed Santa with a sleigh and reindeer. Worrying over this perplexing issue kept her busy until they reached town.

Daddy parked near the grocery store, and all of the children jumped out of the car. Cold air made Janie's lungs hurt, and puffs of vapor floated in the air with each breath she took. Her older brothers set off immediately to do their Christmas shopping and to look for their friends, leaving the two girls and Daddy standing by the car. Daddy looked after them and sighed.

"Go with Margie," Daddy said to Janie. "You can look at dolls while I get groceries. When I finish, I'll come find you."

Margie squared her shoulders in what Jerry called her "martyr look" before taking Janie's mittened hand and leading her down the street. The snow beneath their feet squeaked with each step they took. The little town was poor and did not have sidewalks yet, but boardwalks lined the street, making a hollow sound as the girls walked. Piles of snow almost obscured the hitching rails and water troughs that could still be found in front of a few businesses. The sisters giggled to see Hudsons, Studebakers, Chevys, and Fords parked in front of the troughs as though the automobiles might need a drink while their owners were shopping. A single mule was tied in front of one business that displayed a neon sign in its window.

A sharp wind blew along Main Street, causing the girls to shiver. Janie pulled her scarf higher over her nose and was thankful for the thick wool snow pants, even if they were ugly and had belonged to two boy cousins before being handed down to her. She was glad for her woolly gray coat too. Mama had cut up an old coat of her own to make it for Janie, but it had never belonged to another kid. She loved her coat, even though her brothers claimed it made her look like a fat, gray sheep.

"In here." Margie pointed to a doorway that Janie recognized as the cobbler's shop. She'd been there last summer when Daddy had new heels put on his boots. Neither she nor Margie needed their shoes repaired. She didn't want to go inside the cobbler's shop. What if Santa should come while they were in the shop? She didn't want to miss him and the treat he would bring.

A cold blast of wind brushed her scarf from her face and seemed to cut right through her thick coat. Shoving her hands deep in her pockets, she huddled miserably in the doorway of the shop, undecided whether to venture inside.

The cold won out. Janie figured the cobbler's shop would be better than remaining outdoors any longer. She started to follow Margie through the door.

A movement caught her eye, and she stood transfixed, forgetting how cold she was. In the cobbler's window was a little train. It had a black engine and a coal car; brown, red, and yellow boxcars; and ended with a red caboose. A beam of light shone down the tracks from the tiny engine. It was only a few inches high, but it raced around an oval track and through a mountain tunnel, then emerged to race toward a bridge. A child-size village and miniature farms bordered the tracks. It was the most wonderful thing she'd ever seen.

"Come on, Janie." Margie tugged at her sleeve. "It will be warmer inside."

"But I want to see the train, and what if Santa Claus comes?"

"The firemen will turn on the siren when they start down the street, and there will be plenty of time to hurry outside," Margie assured her from her lofty position of being the older sister. Janie glanced down the street, seeing nothing but snow swirling before gusts of wind and a string of colored lights dancing between two lampposts. She hurried after her sister.

Inside the store, Janie followed Margie's example, stomping snow from her boots then using her teeth to pull her mittens from her hands. The worn mittens dangled from string Mama had attached to them and ran through the sleeves of her coat to keep them from getting lost.

Janie looked around; the cobbler's shop looked different. There were still shoes and boots lining one wall, and a boot rested on the upside-down metal form that looked like a boot anvil—a "last"—which was positioned on a pedestal by the cobbler's stool. Harnesses were draped on another wall, and several saddles rested on sawhorses. But there was also a Christmas tree in one corner. It had brightly colored packages gathered around it.

A sound reminded her of the train. By standing on her toes and resting her chin on the divider that separated the display window from the rest of the room, she could see into the area where the train rushed around in its steady circle. It looked just like a real train only smaller. She wished Santa Claus would bring her a train like that.

"The dolls are this way," Margie whispered, tugging on Janie's hand. Reluctantly, Janie followed her sister to a stairway leading down to a room beneath the cobbler's shop. She looked around in surprise and delight.

"I didn't know there were toys under the cobbler's shop!"

"It's just because Christmas is coming," Margie told her. "The rest of the year the cobbler doesn't use this room. Oh, look, there are the dolls." She hurried toward the display, dragging Janie behind her.

Janie looked at the dolls for several minutes. There was a rubber doll that could be bathed. It had a bottle that a little girl could put water in. That might be fun. But there was a real baby at her house, and Mama sometimes let her feed him a bottle of water. Margie sighed over a doll with real hair that could be brushed and combed. It wore a pretty dress with a pinafore and shoes that could be taken off and put back on. It had its own curlers too. One doll came with a suitcase full of clothes. Janie liked the suitcase, but she wasn't really interested in the dolls.

"Let's look at the other toys." She tugged on Margie's hand.

"Just a minute." Margie continued staring at the doll. "Isn't she beautiful?"

"I guess so." Janie slipped her hand free. She didn't want to look at dolls. There was a display of trucks nearby, and she drifted toward them. As she stood looking at the trucks, two boys stepped between her and the display, pinching her toes and blocking her view. She drifted farther down the aisle, looking at tin dishes, a doll cradle, and a barn with carved animals. There were bicycles and a green tractor with pedals. She'd like to drive that tractor. If it hadn't been placed on a countertop where she couldn't reach it, she'd have given it a try.

She slipped between a large lady and a stack of puzzles and coloring books. Janie liked puzzles, but she didn't stop to look at them. Straight ahead was the staircase. She'd go watch the train until Margie got through looking at the dolls.

On reaching the top of the stairs, she was disappointed to see a group of boys gathered around the partition that separated the window display from the room. Determined to see the train, she wormed her way between long legs until she could see just over the partition to watch the train. A whistle blew, and the train clattered across the bridge. Several of the boys whistled and shouted, but she tuned them out. Her imagination took wing as she dreamed of playing with the little train.

She felt a tug on her sleeve and turned to see Margie with tears running down her cheeks. "I thought you were lost," she whispered.

"I'm not lost. I just got tired of looking at dumb old dolls," she defended herself.

"I was supposed to keep hold of your hand," Margie said, blaming herself for her little sister's disappearance. "And you promised you would mind."

Janie hung her head. She should have told Margie she was going to look at the train. Before she could apologize or Margie could scold her, the fire whistle shrieked.

Margie grabbed Janie's hand and started running toward the door. They had to squirm between all of the other children and their parents who were trying to exit the cobbler's shop. The girls emerged to see the street lined with people who were hurrying from the various businesses along Main Street. Margie wiggled her way between people, towing Janie behind her until they stood at the front of the crowd.

A big, red truck was slowly making its way toward them. A large man in a red suit stood at the back of the truck, waving to the crowd. Janie jumped up and down with excitement. As the fire engine inched closer, she could see a wagonload of barrels, pulled by a team of white horses following the fire truck. Several men stood among the barrels, holding small brown paper bags.

The truck stopped, and Santa climbed down to take up a position close to the wagon. Children poured onto the street. The men on the wagon handed Santa several of the brown bags, which he in turn began distributing to the children. When Margie and Janie got close enough, he thrust two of the little paper sacks toward them. The girls grasped them eagerly before other children pressed between them and Santa.

Janie started to open her sack, but Margie told her to wait until they were back on the boardwalk. Moving against a swarming tide of children, they at last managed to reach the broad planks that served as a walkway. Janie could wait no longer. She thrust her hand inside the bag and felt peanuts. Digging deeper, her hand encountered something smooth. It didn't feel like an orange. She pulled it out and stared in dismay at an apple. There had to be a mistake! She could have an apple anytime. Daddy kept a barrel of apples in the cellar. She looked around for Santa Claus and noticed the other children. Some were holding apples while others held oranges. Tears welled in her eyes. Then her sister reached out to take the bag. Margie carefully folded the top back down and tucked the bag in her pocket. She then handed Janie her own paper bag. Janie peered inside and saw an orange.

She thought she might burst with happiness, but then she looked at Margie. Margie looked like she might cry. Suddenly Janie didn't want the orange. She didn't want Margie to be sad; besides, she was the one who did naughty things and got in trouble.

"You keep it!" She thrust the bag back at her sister.

Margie hesitated then accepted the bag. "Let's take it home to share with Mama and the twins."

"There you are!" Daddy came toward them. He was accompanied by their brothers, each with a paper bag protruding from a coat pocket and a bright orange in hand.

All the way home, Janie could smell the oranges her brothers ate as they lounged in the backseat and whispered amongst themselves. Margie didn't say much, and Janie leaned against the cold car window and wondered how Santa knew she deserved only an apple instead of an orange. Maybe her brothers were right, and on Christmas morning she'd find nothing but a lump of coal in her stocking. Maybe this wasn't going to be the best Christmas ever after all.

"You better get started on chores as soon as we get home." Daddy turned slightly to speak to the boys behind him. "It looks like we might get another snowstorm."

Janie straightened up to peer at the heavy black clouds. She didn't mind if it snowed. She liked snow. She liked making snowmen and forts and tossing snow in the air for the dogs to chase.

Daddy stopped the Willy in front of their mailbox before starting up the long lane that led to their house. He seemed disappointed to find it empty.

Mama fussed with getting Janie's coat and boots off after they entered the house. Margie explained about the orange, and Mama divided it between the two girls, giving their two-year-old brothers each a section.

"I was surprised there was no mail today." Daddy's voice was nonchalant, a sure signal to Janie that she should listen closely. Daddy always tried to hide secrets by making them sound unimportant.

"Oh, it's on the end of the kitchen counter," Mama said in an equally offhand voice. "The mailman brought it to the house."

Aha! The mailman only drove up their lane, honking and waving, when he had a package to deliver, like the baby chicks he brought last spring or Margie's and the big boys' school clothes just before school started. She wondered what he'd brought this time. She almost asked then decided it would do no good. No one ever told her any secrets.

"Your father sent . . ." Mama's voice trailed off, and she looked around to see who might be listening. Janie pretended to be concentrating on getting the snow pants off. She knew her daddy's father lived a long way from Idaho and that it was always warm where he lived. He'd come to visit last summer. He'd brought a funny-smelling lady and her little white dog with him. Her dog wasn't good for much except barking. It was afraid of the sheep and cows, and even old Shep growled at it just like he growled at the cats who tried to steal food from his dish. Janie didn't think Grandpa liked her very much, and his new wife didn't like her at all. They told Daddy he "should do something about that child."

"Nothing else?" Daddy frowned.

"There's still plenty of time." Mama didn't sound like she thought there was plenty of time.

Daddy shrugged his heavy chore coat on and left for the barn while Mama started preparing supper. Margie was playing with the twins, so Janie figured it was the perfect time to peek in Mama's closet. That's where she'd hidden the Easter baskets and Janie's birthday presents, so it seemed the logical place to find whatever her grandfather had sent.

Janie wasn't disappointed. A large wooden crate sat on the floor beneath Mama's dresses. It was nailed shut. She tried to pry it open with the heel of one of Mama's church shoes but was disappointed when she couldn't loosen the nails.

A loud wail erupted behind her, and she looked around to see her baby brother waving his feet and fists as he screamed. She closed the closet door and hurried to the side of his crib.

"Shhh," she whispered through the crib bars, but it was no use.

Mama entered the room and deftly scooped the screaming infant into her arms. The baby stopped howling, and Mama turned to frown at Janie. "What are you doing in here?" she asked.

"I tried to make him stop crying."

"I guess you were trying to help." Mama's face looked tired.

Janie hung her head. She really had tried to make the baby stop crying, but she'd also awakened him in the first place. She hadn't meant to wake him, and she hadn't meant to lie about her reason for being in her parents' bedroom, but Mama would be angry if she explained she'd been looking at the wooden crate Grandpa had sent.

There was snow on Daddy's and her brothers' coats when they returned from doing their chores.

"I think we're in for a bad one," Daddy said as he sat down at the head of the table. "It's probably a good thing I got groceries today."

Janie glanced toward the window and was surprised to see it was already covered with snow. It was still snowing when she and Margie snuggled down in their bed that night, and it was still snowing when she awoke the next morning.

It took a long time for Daddy and her brothers to do their chores in the morning, because they had to dig a path to the barn. When they finally returned, Daddy said they'd have to hold Sunday School at home that morning. There weren't any roads open, and the snow was too deep for the Willy.

The snow continued to fall all day, and when Monday morning came, her brothers woke her with cheers because they'd just heard on the radio that school had been canceled until the storm ended and roads could be cleared. They groaned and complained when Daddy told them that with no school, they'd have plenty of time to shovel the trail to the barn again.

Janie thought being snowed in would be lots of fun, but it just made everyone cranky. The twins whined and messed up her paper dolls. When she scolded them, Daddy sent her to her room. There was nothing to do in the tiny room, which held just a bed for the two girls and a dresser for their clothes. Then she spied Margie's new coloring book on top of the dresser.

Margie yelled at her for coloring pictures in her coloring book, and her brothers grumbled about all the snow they had to shovel while the girls did nothing. Mama paced the floor and at frequent intervals peered through the window toward the end of the lane. Finally

Daddy took Jerry and Ron with him to put runners on the hay wagon so they could haul feed to the sheep and cattle that weren't close to the barn. Janie wanted to help, but Daddy said she'd just be in the way.

By early afternoon, the snow had stopped falling. Giving in to her pleas, Mama allowed Janie to put on her coat and the hated snow pants to go outside for a short time. She sent Ralph with her to keep an eye on her. Ralph objected, but once they were outside, he laughed when he saw that the snow on either side of the path was higher than Janie's head. It gave him an idea.

Together the children began burrowing a tunnel into the snow from the trench-like path that led to the barn. Their tunnel wound deep beneath a large drift that had formed at one corner of the house.

"I don't think it's safe to play under all that snow," Mama said when she discovered their tunnel. "Janie, it's time for you to go inside and get warm. Ralph, would you see if the mail has come?"

"The road hasn't been plowed. The mailman can't come today," Ralph protested.

"Yes, you're probably right. You'd better come in now too." Reluctantly the children followed her inside the house. Janie noticed that until dark, Mama made frequent trips to the kitchen window to stare down the lane to where the mailbox sat with its tall cap of snow. It seemed to Janie that Mama was sad and worrying about something.

The next morning when Janie awoke, the house seemed especially quiet. Only a faint light shone from the hall. She lay still, listening to the quiet until she remembered it was Christmas Eve. She couldn't stay in bed, wasting any of the day before Christmas. Christmas Eve was almost as exciting as Christmas Day. All day there would be secrets, and mysterious packages would appear beneath the Christmas tree in the front room. Mama would make pancakes for supper, and then the whole family would gather around the tree to give each other presents. Then it would be off to bed before Santa Claus arrived and found anyone still awake.

Slipping from bed, she padded on bare feet to the front room. Mama laid her clothes out by the oil heater in the front room each winter morning so they would be warm when she put them on. As Janie neared the kitchen door, she heard voices. Mama and Daddy were talking so softly she could barely hear them.

"There's at least another foot of snow," Daddy said. "With more than four feet of snow and the roads drifted over, the mail isn't going to get through today."

"What about the horses?"

"It's too far, and the snow is too deep for even the best horse to make it to town and back in less than two days."

"What are we going to tell the kids? The older boys will understand, but how do we explain to the younger ones that Santa isn't coming this year?"

Santa wasn't coming? Janie saw Mama wipe at her eyes with a corner of her apron. Janie stumbled backward. This wasn't going to be the best Christmas ever. Silently she crept back to her bed and slid beneath the big quilt that covered the bed she shared with Margie. She screwed her eyes shut and rolled herself into a tight ball of misery. It couldn't be true. Mama was wrong. Santa Claus would come. Snow wouldn't make any difference to Santa's sleigh. Just because Mr. Petersen couldn't drive his car in the snow to deliver the mail didn't mean Santa's sleigh and reindeer couldn't fly right over the snow.

An awful thought entered her head. Snow couldn't be the reason Santa Claus wasn't coming. It was because she, Janie, had been bad. Tears rolled down her cheeks. She didn't mean to be bad. She never meant to break things or lose them, and if the twins would leave her things alone, she wouldn't have to take them back and make the little boys cry.

Everyone said she needed to be more careful. She should share better. She should help more. Even Santa thought she was naughty; he'd given her an apple instead of the orange she'd wanted so badly. It was her fault Santa Claus wasn't coming. She had to do something.

Once more, Janie slid out of bed. This time she went straight to the heater to collect her clothing and dress herself. She set the table without Mama asking. After breakfast, she played with the twins and remembered not to yell at them.

"Girls," Mama said as she knelt beside the wooden crate dollhouse where Janie and Margie were arranging the paper dolls they'd cut from the catalog. She twisted her apron and bit her lip before going on. "This storm has been really bad. It doesn't look like Santa Claus will be able to come tonight. It might be next week before Santa will be able to come."

"But his sleigh is only magic on Christmas Eve!" Margie looked stricken; tears slipped down her cheeks.

Janie didn't cry. It was too late to be good. She wished she could comfort Margie and tell her the truth. It wasn't the storm; it was her. Santa Claus wasn't coming because Janie hadn't been good enough. It wasn't fair! Santa should still bring presents for Margie and baby David—maybe the twins too because they were little and didn't know better.

"It looks like you won't even get a lump of coal in your sock, Janie," Ron announced as he and Janie's other older brothers came in from feeding the sheep, where Daddy must have given them the same message Mama had given the girls.

*The Spirit of Christmas: Stories of the Season*

"Janie ain't gittin' nuttin' for Christmas," the boys caroled. "'Cause she ain't been nuttin' but bad."

"You ain't either!" she shouted back. With her small fists on her hips, she glared at her brothers. Daddy intervened before she could accuse them of being as bad as she was and tell them that Santa's decision not to stop at their house was as much their fault as hers.

"Stop your teasing," he ordered the boys. "We'll still have Christmas. There are our presents for each other under the tree, we'll read the Christmas story tonight, and Mama will roast a goose with dressing tomorrow." He might have said more, but the telephone rang.

The telephone made just one extra-long, shrill ring instead of the usual series of shorts and longs that signaled whether her parents or a neighbor should pick up the telephone. Mama and Daddy exchanged worried looks, then Daddy reached for the phone.

"Hello!" he shouted. An echo of voices sounded from the receiver that Janie could hear clearly. Everyone on their party line seemed to have answered the strange ring. Daddy was quiet for several minutes, and Janie could hear the rumble of a man's voice but couldn't understand his words.

"Roland tried getting out with his tractor. It got stuck before he got to the end of his lane. I've got runners on my hay wagon," Daddy said. "I'll start as soon as I can get my team harnessed and meet everyone at the end of Courtney's lane." He hung up and turned to Mama with a sparkle in his eyes.

"The county is plowing the highway. Peterson from the post office said he should be able to get as far as Aiklie's corner by four o'clock."

"Do you want me to go with you?" Jerry offered.

"No, Virgil and Clark will be here by the time I get the team harnessed and the horses' legs wrapped. We'll meet the others at Courtney's and take turns breaking the crust on the drifts for the horses. Courtney said the wind has swept that long stretch between his place and Joe's almost clean, so if we cut across the fields, we should reach the highway by four."

"Be careful," Mama cautioned as she wrapped a scarf around Daddy's neck. Janie couldn't tell if the tears in Mama's eyes were because she didn't want Daddy to go or because she was happy he was going to get the mail. It seemed like a lot of fuss to drive the horses six miles to the highway through snow too deep for the Willy or the school bus just to get the mail when Mama always said they never got anything but bills.

"Start the chores a little early," Daddy advised Janie's brothers before going out the door. "I don't know what time I'll be back."

The afternoon stretched into evening, and darkness came early. Mama fussed with warming the boys up when they came in from doing chores. She went to the window often to pull the curtain aside so she could peer out. An air of suppressed excitement mixed with anxiety seemed to hover about Mama and the boys as they popped a big bowl of popcorn and Mama read the Christmas story from St. Luke. The story didn't make Janie feel any better. She suspected Jesus wasn't any more pleased with her than Santa Claus was. She almost never sat still on her chair in Sunday School or raised her hand before shouting out the answers to her teachers' questions.

"Hang your stockings," Mama told the children, "then off to bed with you."

It seemed pretty silly to Janie to hang up her stocking when Santa Claus wasn't coming, but she obediently draped her sock over the line behind the oil heater where Mama hung clothes to dry when it was too stormy to hang them outside.

When all of the children except Jerry were ready for bed, Mama led them in prayers. Janie wasn't sure why Jerry got to stay up, even if he was the oldest, but it was probably to help Daddy with the horses when he came. She lay awake in her bed for a long time. From the living room drifted the sound of Christmas carols interspersed with liberal amounts of static coming from the radio. Once she thought she heard the jingle of sleigh bells, but she dismissed the thought at once. Santa Claus wasn't coming.

\* \* \*

"Janie! Wake up!" Margie pulled at the covers. "Santa Claus came!"

*Could it be true?* Janie blinked owlishly then bolted from bed to dash into the living room. She stopped in awe. Eight mysterious piles of toys and clothes circled the tree. Her bulging stocking rested atop one of those piles. There was the inevitable doll and new underwear, but there was also clay, a kaleidoscope, a book, a whistle that looked like a bird, and a jigsaw puzzle. There was a new dress Mama had made for her; her brothers had given her a box of cherry chocolates; and from Margie she had received a Life Savers book just like the one she'd picked out for Margie.

There was something round in the toe of her stocking. With eager hands she dumped the contents of the sock on the linoleum floor. She stared past the nuts and candy to the dimpled orange. When she gathered it up and ran to the kitchen to show Mama, she almost stumbled over the crate that had come a week ago from Grandpa in far-off California. It was open and nearly full of oranges.

Janie hurried back to the living room to inspect Margie's and her brothers' gifts before settling beside her own with a troubled sigh. She was glad she wasn't on Santa's naughty list after all—or was she? Maybe he was just giving her a second chance. She wasn't very good at second chances, or thirds. She sat up straight. She loved everything about Christmas, and she'd come awfully close to losing out on this one. She'd be really good until next Christmas. She wouldn't break anything or take things away from the twins, and she'd—

"Where did that frown come from?" Mama sat beside Janie and pulled her onto her lap. "Don't you like your presents?"

"I love my presents." She hugged Mama and felt a fat tear slide down her cheek. "But Santa Claus almost didn't come because I was naughty, so I'm going to do everything right from now on so he'll come again next year. I won't make any more mistakes."

"I'm glad you want to be good." Mama laughed. "But everyone makes mistakes, and sometimes accidents just happen. Santa didn't almost miss us because of you."

"We didn't know you really believed that stuff we said." Ralph looked aghast. Janie was surprised to see the whole family gathered around her, looking worried.

"We were just teasing," Ron added.

"'Cause you're so much fun to tease," Jerry said.

"You can play with my doll. She has real hair," Margie offered.

Janie saw something in the faces gathered around her she hadn't noticed before. Her family loved her, even when she made mistakes. Grandpa in California loved her; he'd sent oranges. Santa Claus must love her too, because he'd changed his mind about skipping her house. She had a feeling that Baby Jesus loved her too. This really was the best Christmas ever.

# THE HAGGERTY CHRISTMAS MIRACLE
## BY BETSY BRANNON GREEN

Eugenia Atkins and her little dog, Lady, were taking their regular morning walk through Haggerty, Georgia, on what promised to be a beautiful, warm December day. Haggerty was an unremarkable town by the world's standards, but for seventy-eight years it had been the center of Eugenia's universe. She was born there, she would die there, and in between she would make it her business to look out for the town's other 5,963 residents.

Distracted by the nice weather, Eugenia allowed Lady to venture farther than usual. As they walked, Eugenia mentally reviewed her Christmas preparations. She had purchased her gifts, mailed out her cards, and visited the aged or infirm. Now she could relax and enjoy the holidays. Her mind touched briefly on her husband, Charles, who had been dead for over five years now. Although she still missed him, she had learned to enjoy life alone.

She was startled from her reverie by the sound of barking dogs. Eugenia blinked and studied her surroundings. She and Lady had walked all the way to the western edge of town, near the home of Dub Shaw. Dub had graduated from high school the same year as Eugenia, but the two of them had never been what she would consider friends.

Throughout his life Dub had struggled with a dependence on alcohol, and after his house burned down under suspicious circumstances, he'd spent a few months in the local assisted-living facility. Once he had his drinking problem under control, he had hired a local contractor to bulldoze the charred remains of his old house and install a double-wide mobile home on the foundation. He lived there now with his pack of mongrel dogs—which Eugenia assumed were attracting Lady.

Dub had never been particularly pleasant, and now that he was sober he was downright cranky. Anxious to avoid a lengthy discussion of all Dub's complaints against society, Eugenia turned around and headed back toward town. "Come on, Lady," she instructed the dog. "It's time we went home."

Lady was usually very obedient, so Eugenia was surprised when the dog continued down the road toward Dub's house.

"Lady!" Eugenia called after the dog sharply. "You come here right now!"

Lady ignored Eugenia, running as fast as her short little legs would carry her.

"The very idea!" Eugenia muttered to herself. Then she marched with purpose down the road after her disobedient dog.

Eugenia was breathless by the time she caught up with Lady. The dog was barking happily and running in circles around the feet of two children who were playing in the yard of a small house on the edge of Dub's property. For as long as Eugenia could remember the house had been vacant—used only for storing hay during the winter. Putting up a hand to shield her eyes against the sun, she studied the house. It was still a sorry sight, but some small improvements were visible, and there was light coming through the windows—indicating that the occupants now had electricity inside.

The older child kneeled in the brown grass to pet Lady. "What's her name?" he asked Eugenia.

"Her name is Lady, and she's in big trouble," Eugenia said with a fierce look at the little dog.

Lady barked cheerfully.

"What's your name?" the boy questioned further.

"My name is Miss Eugenia Atkins," Eugenia replied. "What's yours?"

*The Spirit of Christmas: Stories of the Season*

"I'm Ethan," the older boy said and then waved toward his brother, who was vigorously sucking his thumb. "And this is Evan. I'm six and he's four."

Eugenia nodded in acknowledgment. "It's nice to meet both of you."

"Is something wrong?" a voice asked.

Eugenia looked up to see a young woman emerge from the house. As she rushed toward them, Eugenia noted the sweat pants and large T-shirt stretched to the limits across the woman's protruding stomach. She estimated that the boys would be joined by another sibling in approximately two months.

"Nothing's wrong," Eugenia assured the boys' mother. "We're all just getting acquainted. I'm Eugenia Atkins, and I live on Maple Street—so we're distant neighbors."

The woman's face relaxed into a relieved smile. "I'm Carrie Carter."

Eugenia looked around at the ramshackle house and weed-ridden lawn. "I didn't realize anyone was living here."

"We moved in a couple of weeks ago," Carrie explained. "My husband, Len, will graduate from the Georgia School of Medicine in May, and he's doing his clinicals in Albany. Since our student loans are already . . ." Carrie paused, searching for the appropriate word. She finally settled on, "*daunting*, I asked

Uncle Dub if we could live here until Len's through with school."

"Uncle Dub?" Eugenia repeated.

Carrie smiled. "Well, he's not really my uncle. My grandmother Eunice was his cousin, but we always called him Uncle Dub. I knew he had a vacant house on his land." Carrie's eyes strayed back to her home. "It's in a little worse shape than I remembered, but at least we don't have to pay rent."

"That's only a good arrangement if the roof doesn't fall in on you," Eugenia remarked.

Apparently Carrie thought this was a joke, because she laughed.

"We're not in a financial position to do much—but we're trying to make it as habitable as possible."

"And I helped my dad patch the roof," Ethan informed Eugenia proudly.

*A fairy godmother with a magic wand wouldn't be able to make that house habitable*, Eugenia thought. To Ethan she said, "I'm glad to hear that you are a helpful boy. So many children these days are spoiled and lazy."

"I'm helpful too," four-year-old Evan said around his grimy thumb. "Not lazy."

Eugenia gave the little boy a smile. "That's good." Then she addressed his mother. "You really should try to break him of that thumb-sucking habit. There's no telling what kind of germs he's introducing into his system and all the while misaligning his teeth."

"I've tried to get him to stop," Carrie said. "But my nagging just seems to make it worse."

"One of my nephews sucked his thumb," Eugenia informed her. "I dipped his thumb in pepper juice and told him it was poison. It broke him of the habit."

Carrie's eyes widened.

"Sometimes you have to use drastic measures for their own good." Eugenia's impromptu parenting lesson was interrupted by Ethan.

"Can I show Lady my room?" he asked his mother.

Carrie smiled. "Of course. Miss Eugenia, won't you and Lady come inside?"

Eugenia was curious, so she accepted the invitation. The children led the way into the house with Lady at their heels. Eugenia was disappointed to see that if anything, the interior of the house was worse than the exterior—not to mention that it still smelled like wet hay.

Carrie indicated a couple of buckets on the floor in the entryway. "The roof only leaks when it rains."

Eugenia frowned. "I thought Ethan said your husband patched the roof."

"Len does what he can, but he's a doctor, not a carpenter."

The children ran down the hallway and into the open door of a bedroom. Eugenia glanced to the right into the tiny living room. It was furnished with a sagging couch and two folding chairs. The couch was covered with a blanket, and Eugenia could only imagine the condition of the upholstery underneath. In the far corner of the room was a bedraggled pine tree that looked like it had been cut at random from a roadside.

Carrie confirmed this with her next comment. "Don't you love our tree?" She pointed at the pitiful specimen. "We couldn't afford to buy one, so Uncle Dub let us cut a tree from off his property."

Eugenia reexamined the tree and nodded. It looked like something Dub would grow.

"The kids and I have been making our own ornaments." Carrie pointed at a round disc of plastic. "This angel is made from a Cool Whip lid," she said, as if this fact weren't perfectly obvious.

Eugenia forced herself to smile at the tacky ornament. "I love angels."

"Can I get you some coffee?" Carrie offered as they entered the small kitchen.

Eugenia took in the well-worn linoleum floor and the faded wallpaper. "No, thank you."

Carrie sat in one of the chairs that encircled the kitchen table, and Eugenia sat in another. "How is your grandmother?" Eugenia inquired politely.

"Deceased," Carried replied. "My parents too."

"I'm sorry."

"Me too," Carrie acknowledged with a small sigh.

Eugenia let her eyes drift around the gloomy kitchen. "So will you be spending the holidays with your husband's parents?"

"No," Carrie replied. "We don't have a car, and Len's parents live in Florida. They don't have room for all of us, and the kids make them nervous."

Eugenia frowned in disapproval. "I've never particularly cared for my two nephews, but they're always welcome in my house at Christmas."

Carrie laughed. "I'd rather stay here than waste most of our holiday traveling. Besides, Ethan and Evan are old enough for us to begin our own Christmas traditions. I want them to be able to hang their stockings on our fireplace and wake up in their own beds on Christmas morning."

Eugenia didn't see how waking up in this house could be considered a good thing on *any* day, let alone Christmas.

"This will be my first chance to bake a turkey," Carrie was continuing cheerfully. "I'm really looking forward to the challenge."

Finally an opportunity to offer practical assistance. "I've baked many turkeys during my life, and I'd be glad to help you."

"I might take you up on that," Carrie said. "I want my first turkey to be a success, but mostly I'm looking forward to all of us being together for a few days. Len is taking his final exams now, and his job ends tomorrow night. Then we can sit around and enjoy the holidays."

"Where does your husband work?"

"He's a waiter at the Rawhide Steakhouse in Albany."

Eugenia nodded. "I've eaten there before. The food's good, but the lighting is terrible."

Carrie laughed. "They call that *atmosphere*."

"I call it annoying."

Carrie was still smiling as she said, "Annoying atmosphere or not, that job has been such a blessing to us. Len has earned enough money to buy the boys each a couple of toys, and he's getting me a suitcase so I don't have to borrow one when I go to the hospital to have the baby." Her eyes twinkled as she leaned closer. "I'm not supposed to know about that."

Eugenia nodded in approval. "It's hard to keep secrets from a smart wife."

"Especially a wife who religiously studies store receipts hoping to find an error in our favor!"

"I always check my receipts and often find errors," Eugenia confided. "And what are you giving your husband?"

"I found an antique doctor's bag at a flea market for ten dollars." Her glance moved to the sewing machine set up on the small kitchen table. "I'm also making him a new lab coat."

*The Spirit of Christmas: Stories of the Season*

"I'm sure he'll be very pleased."

Carrie blew a stray lock of hair from her eyes. "The kids are making their own gifts for him, too, and I've never seen them so excited. I hope we can finish them up tonight before Len gets home. Then we're going to string some popcorn for the tree and make a star out of aluminum foil."

Eugenia thought about the box of leftover decorations she had at home. "I have some extra ornaments," she told Carrie. "I'd be glad for you to use them if you'd like."

Carrie smiled. "That's very kind."

"What's kind?" Ethan demanded as the children returned with Lady in tow.

"Miss Eugenia said she has some Christmas ornaments we can borrow," his mother explained.

Ethan seemed confused by this. "But we already have ornaments."

Carrie gave her son a meaningful look. "We can't have too many ornaments."

Eugenia reached down and scooped Lady into her arms. "Well, I guess we'd better go." She stood and inched toward the door. "Lady and I will stop by this afternoon with those ornaments."

Carrie and the children followed her to the door. "We'll look forward to that. We don't get many visitors out this way."

As Eugenia left the Carters behind, Lady whimpered. "Don't worry," Eugenia told the little dog. "We'll see them again soon."

During the walk back into town, Eugenia mentally inventoried the extra ornaments she had at home, hoping they would be enough to improve the Carters' tree. Then it occurred to her that almost everyone had Christmas things that they didn't use every year. With a little effort she could probably collect enough Christmas finery to turn the Carters' ramshackle house into a holiday marvel. Well, almost.

The Carters were obviously a deserving family in need of help. After shifting Lady to her other arm, Eugenia picked up her pace. She was now a woman with a mission.

\* \* \*

While she walked, Eugenia used her cell phone to call her sister, Annabelle, who lived in Albany. When Annabelle answered, Eugenia asked, "Do you remember Eunice Shaw?"

"Dub's cousin? Of course I remember her," Annabelle responded. "You're the one who's senile—not me."

Eugenia wanted Annabelle's help, so she chose to ignore this. "Well, I just met her granddaughter, all grown up with a family of her own. She's living in the hay house out on the edge of Dub's place." Eugenia explained about the Carters' destitute circumstances and her plans to improve their holiday season before asking, "Don't you have an extra artificial tree?"

"Yes," Annabelle confirmed. "But I thought you said the family already had a tree."

"They do," Eugenia replied. "But it's a sorry sight. My original plan was to add a lot of ornaments—hoping to cover the tree up. But now I think it would be best to start fresh. Bring it along with any other decorations you want to donate and meet me at the Iversons' house as soon as possible." She hung up without giving Annabelle a chance to disagree and walked as fast as her old legs would carry her.

When Eugenia reached her home on Maple Street, she didn't even pause but marched next door straight up to the Iversons' house.

"Hellooooo!" she called out as she let herself in.

The Iverson children, Emily and Charles, came running and met Eugenia at the door to the kitchen.

"Hey, Miss Eugenia!" Emily greeted.

"Hey, Lady!" Charles added, scooping the little dog up into his arms.

"Hey yourselves," Eugenia said as she hugged them both.

"Mama made pancakes for breakfast, and we have extra," Emily said. "You want some?"

Eugenia walked on into the kitchen where Kate and Mark were seated at the table. "I don't mind if I do."

"Can we play with Lady?" Charles asked.

"You may," Eugenia replied as she took a plate from the cupboard and a fork from the drawer and settled in an empty chair across from the Iversons.

"Morning," she told them as she forked several pancakes onto her plate.

"Good morning to you," Kate Iverson said with a smile. "Would you like some orange juice?"

"Is it fresh?" Eugenia inquired.

"Fresh from the jug," Kate returned.

It never ceased to amaze Eugenia how often young people today chose convenience over quality. "I guess that will have to do." While Kate poured the juice, Eugenia looked up at Mark. "Why aren't you at work? Is it an FBI holiday or something?"

"Officially, I'm on vacation," Mark replied.

"But he's actually working from home," Kate added happily. "Being important does have its drawbacks, like long hours and endless paperwork."

Eugenia narrowed her eyes at Kate. "You seem awful cheery about Mark's long hours. Have the two of you finally gotten sick of each other like a normal married couple?"

*The Spirit of Christmas: Stories of the Season*

Kate laughed. "No." She exchanged a quick glance with Mark and then leaned forward. "But we do have some news."

"You're not moving?" It was Eugenia's greatest fear.

"No," Kate assured her with a smile. "We're going to have a new addition to our family."

Kate had grieved over her inability to have more children ever since Charles was born. Adoption papers had been filed months ago, and Kate's radiant expression suggested that the process was complete. "You're adopting a baby," Eugenia whispered.

"Not exactly," Kate corrected. "But sort of."

Now Eugenia was confused. "How do you 'sort of' adopt a baby?"

"Have you ever heard of 'safe harbor'?" Mark asked.

"Doesn't that mean that during a storm ports will allow almost any ship to dock—even enemies?" Eugenia replied, a forkful of pancakes poised halfway to her mouth.

Mark nodded. "That's what it meant a hundred years ago."

"Don't get smart with me, young man," she advised. "And just what does it mean now?"

"Now the term has several meanings," Mark said with a smile, "one of which refers to the safe disposal of unwanted babies."

Eugenia gasped. "*Disposal* of babies?"

"Maybe *disposal* was a poor choice of words," Mark amended. "If a mother—for whatever reason—finds herself unwilling or unable to care for a newborn, she can drop it off at a safe harbor location without risk of prosecution."

"Places like police stations and hospitals are designated as safe harbors," Kate continued. "The red tape involved in adopting one of these babies is not as lengthy as it is in regular adoptions. So we've applied and qualified."

"Then you're going to adopt one of these abandoned babies?"

"Maybe, probably." Kate looked at Mark again.

"The more pressing issue than finding parents for these babies is finding a place that they can go to until an adoption can be arranged. They need foster families who can be ready to take a baby at a moment's notice."

Kate took up the dialogue. "I've investigated the program thoroughly, and I feel sure that this is what the Lord wants us to do. Eventually we'll probably adopt, but for now we'll provide shelter and comfort for these babies who start life with nothing—not even love." Kate had to pause to wipe tears from her eyes. "My nursery is all set up so I'm ready at *less* than a moment's notice."

Eugenia smiled. "I think that's wonderful. And you know I'm always available to help."

Kate smiled back. "I do know that."

There was a knock at the back door, followed by Annabelle's voice calling, "Good morning!"

"Come on in," Kate invited.

Annabelle appeared in the doorway moments later and breathlessly demanded, "Eugenia, what do you want me to do with this Christmas tree? I've lugged it from the car, and I'm not taking it another inch."

Kate looked between the two sisters and asked, "Christmas tree?"

Eugenia waved toward the table. "Have a seat, Annabelle." Then she briefly described the Carters and their situation.

Kate was instantly sympathetic. "Those poor people. What can we do to help?"

Eugenia was pleased by the offer. "Well, I was thinking that you could mention it to some people at church and see if they have any toys or clothes or furniture that they'd like to donate."

Annabelle raised her eyebrows. "And how are you planning to deliver these donations?"

Eugenia smirked at her sister. "I'm glad you asked. I'm going to arrange for Carrie to come on Thursday morning so I can help her prepare her turkey, to ensure that she will be home. I'll ask Whit to rent a U-Haul truck and round up a couple of teenagers. He'll come here and you'll supervise while they load the donations onto the truck. Then you'll all come and transform Dub's hay house into a Christmas paradise."

"What if they don't want us to transform their house?" Mark asked.

Eugenia waved this aside. "Why would they refuse improvements?"

"I really think it would be best to ask," Mark insisted.

Eugenia was annoyed. "But that would spoil the surprise!"

Before Mark could counter this statement further, there was a knock on the front door.

He went to answer the door, and Annabelle remarked, "Your house is a busy place this morning."

"Miss Eugenia always attracts a crowd," Kate murmured as Mark returned with George Ann Simmons. Kate pasted on a welcome smile and said, "Hey, Miss George Ann."

"Good morning," George Ann replied.

Annabelle returned the greeting, but Eugenia couldn't make herself do more than nod. George Ann was a nuisance, and her presence reduced the morning from 'good' to just 'fair,' in Eugenia's opinion.

"Would you care for some pancakes?" Kate said.

"I've already eaten, thank you," George Ann declined. Then she further ruined the day by turning to Eugenia and saying, "I told Polly to meet me at your house so we could all walk to bell choir practice together, but you weren't there."

No amount of practice would improve Haggerty's bell choir—an organization Eugenia participated in only because George Ann had bribed her into joining. And she resented the insinuation that she should have her daily activities approved by George Ann in advance. "I see you tracked me down like a bloodhound, though," Eugenia muttered.

George Ann either missed or ignored the intended jab. "I figured you'd be here, and I'm sure Polly saw me walk over, so she should be here soon."

No one argued this point. Polly was a dedicated busybody and missed little of what happened in the neighborhood.

"And why is there a Christmas tree in the driveway?" George Ann wanted to know.

Kate summed up the Carters' plight and the plans they'd made to remedy the situation. At the conclusion of Kate's explanation, George Ann surprised even Eugenia with her complaint. "It's unfair of you and the Mormons to help these people. After all, they do live in Haggerty, so the churches here should have the opportunity."

"That's ridiculous," Eugenia scoffed. "As long as the Carters get the help they need, it doesn't matter who provides the assistance."

Polly rushed into the kitchen just in time to hear this remark. "Why are we all at the Iversons' house, and who needs assistance?" she asked.

"A young couple with two children is living in that hay house on the edge of Dub Shaw's property," George Ann informed Polly. "They need help, but Eugenia and the Iversons are trying to keep us from doing our Christian duty."

Polly gave Eugenia a disappointed look. "Eugenia, you know how much I love to do my Christian duty!"

Eugenia did know, and this kept her from chastising Polly. Instead she turned her wrath toward George Ann. "I found them, and I'm going to help them have a wonderful Christmas. Now why don't the two of you just go on and ring bells and leave us alone."

"From what you've said, there's enough need to go around," Mark suggested in a conciliatory tone.

Annabelle jumped straight onto his bandwagon. "Just imagine the improvements that could be made if the whole town—Mormons, Baptists, and Methodists—all joined forces. Why, it would be a Christmas miracle that would be talked about for years to come!"

*The Spirit of Christmas: Stories of the Season*

Eugenia didn't want to include George Ann, but she did want the Carters to have the best Christmas possible. So she nodded. "I guess the Baptists and Methodists can help if they want to."

"I'll bet people all over town would donate furniture and clothing," Kate suggested. "And maybe we could get some local merchants to donate the supplies to properly repair the roof."

"The last time I saw that house it was in terrible shape," Annabelle interrupted. "I know you all mean well, but honestly, if we're trying to improve the Carters' living conditions, we should just move them somewhere else."

"Well, obviously we can't do that," George Ann said.

Eugenia hated to agree with George Ann, but she had no choice. "Obviously we can't fix everything that's wrong with the house in one day," she looked at her sister, "and we *certainly* can't move the Carters out of their home on Christmas Eve. But if they have a new roof, at least they won't need to worry about leaks."

"Jack Gamble is our elders quorum president," Mark said and received blank looks from everyone except Kate and Eugenia. "An elders quorum president is the Mormon equivalent of a roofing expert," he explained with a smile. "I'm sure he can get the materials donated and round up plenty of volunteers to roof the Carters' house."

Eugenia beamed at him. "So the Mormons will provide a new roof. We still need furniture and decorations and gifts and clothes—"

"And toys!" Polly chimed in gleefully.

"And toys," Eugenia agreed.

Kate took a notebook out of a kitchen drawer and sat down at the table. "Okay, who's going to do what?"

Once each of the Carters' needs had been assigned to the various religious organizations, Eugenia allowed herself to be dragged to bell choir practice. An ear-splitting hour later she returned home and gathered an assortment of Christmas tree ornaments. Then she and Lady drove out to the Carters' house to make a delivery and set the Christmas miracle in motion.

\* \* \*

When Eugenia parked her old Buick in front of Dub Shaw's old hay house, it looked even worse than she remembered. Eugenia was doubly thankful that she'd taken matters into her own hands as she crossed the lawn to knock on the front door. Ethan and Evan were thrilled to see Lady, and Carrie accepted the box of ornaments with a grateful smile.

"I can't thank you enough," she said.

*And there's plenty more of that ahead,* Eugenia thought to herself. Out loud she said, "I thought I might come by on Thursday morning and help you get your turkey ready to bake."

"Oh, I hate to bother you on Christmas Eve," Carrie said. "I'm sure I can handle the turkey by myself."

Eugenia knew that Carrie was more concerned about protecting her family time than the turkey. But this was crucial to the plan's success, so Eugenia pressed on. "I don't mind at all. In fact, I'd be glad for something to do. Since my husband died, the holidays have been a little lonely."

Carrie chewed her lower lip. "Well . . ."

Eugenia could tell that Carrie was weakening and pulled out all the stops. "It would mean so much to me."

Carrie sighed in defeat. "I'd be glad for your help."

Eugenia tried not to let her satisfaction show. "I'll be here at ten o'clock on Thursday morning."

\* \* \*

By Wednesday afternoon, Eugenia's house was full to overflowing with contributions for the Carters, so she called Brother Watty, the Methodist preacher, and arranged to store the items at the Family Life building until Thursday. A moving crew composed of a Boy

Scout troop and two gravediggers from the Haggerty Mortuary used U-Haul trucks rented by Eugenia's beau, Whit Owens, to transfer all the donations.

Then Eugenia, Polly, and Kate began the overwhelming task of determining what the Carters could actually use and what should be taken to the Goodwill. They were about halfway through when Annabelle arrived carrying a huge box.

"I declare!" Eugenia cried. "What is that?"

"It's an artificial tree for the Carters," Annabelle replied as she placed the box on the floor.

"You already brought your old one," Kate reminded her.

"I know," Annabelle acknowledged. "But since we're trying to make this the most special Christmas ever, I stopped by The Santa Shoppe in Albany. When I saw this tree, I knew the Carters had to have it."

Eugenia studied the picture of the silver tree on the box. "Is this one of those gaudy aluminum trees like the ones we had in the sixties?"

Annabelle nodded. "It's similar, but it's new and improved. Now they call it *retro*."

Eugenia squinted at the price tag. "Tell me you didn't spend $230 on that tree."

Annabelle shrugged. "Okay, I won't tell you. The woman at The Santa Shoppe said it's all the rage this year."

"The woman at The Santa Shoppe knew a sucker when she saw one," Eugenia murmured.

Annabelle ignored this. "There's a revolving colored light included at no extra charge."

The tree discussion was interrupted by the arrival of George Ann Simmons. She placed a dusty box on the floor beside Annabelle's outrageously expensive Christmas tree and said, "I went through the attic and found some of my father's clothes. They are high quality and still have plenty of good use left in them. So I'm donating them to Mr. Carter."

Eugenia doubted that even someone as poor as Len Carter would considering wearing clothes that had once belonged to George Ann's late father, but she forced herself to say, "How generous."

"I like to do my part," George Ann said.

"Then why don't you stay and help us sort through this stuff," Eugenia suggested.

"Oh, I would," George Ann assured her, "but I have a prior engagement."

As they watched George Ann leave, Eugenia whispered, "Prior engagement, hah! She just said that to get out of doing any actual work!"

"She did donate some of her father's things," Polly pointed out.

Eugenia wasn't impressed. "A few moth-eaten discards!"

"But she holds her father in such high regard," Polly insisted. "So giving away his things is quite a sacrifice—even if they aren't fit to wear."

Annabelle laughed at this remark. "Oh, Polly, you can put a positive spin on anything!"

"Back to work!" Eugenia commanded. "My arthritis is killing me, and if I don't get home and into bed soon, I won't be able to get out of bed tomorrow—let alone surprise the Carters with a Christmas miracle."

Two hours later, Mark called. He insisted that they stop for the night whether they were finished or not. "We're done," Kate assured him. "And I'll be home in a few minutes."

Eugenia confirmed that her helpers could come the next morning when Whit and his moving crew returned. "You'll have to watch them closely to be sure they load the right stuff."

Annabelle, Kate, and Polly all nodded wearily. "You just go to the Carters' house and pretend to cook the turkey. We'll handle Whit and the movers," Annabelle promised.

They were locking the Family Life center's front door when Whit Owens pulled up to the curb driving a minivan.

Eugenia walked over and examined the vehicle. Then she told Whit, "This isn't your usual style."

*The Spirit of Christmas: Stories of the Season*

He smiled. "I'm contributing it to your Christmas cause."

Whit had plenty of money, so the contribution didn't come at any great sacrifice. But Eugenia deeply appreciated his support of her project and knew the van would help the Carters as much as, if not more than, all the other contributions combined.

"I don't know what to say," she said around the lump of emotion that had formed in her throat.

"Just say you'll go out to dinner with me."

"Not tonight," she said. "If it's true that you're as young as you feel—then I'm about two hundred."

He laughed. "Okay, but remember, you owe me a date." He climbed out of the van and handed her the keys. "Can you give me a ride home?"

\* \* \*

Eugenia arrived at the Carters' home a few minutes before ten o'clock on Thursday morning. Carrie opened the door looking tired.

She put a finger to her lips and whispered, "The boys and Len are still asleep. They stayed up late last night finishing their Christmas gifts."

Eugenia felt a momentary pang of guilt for dragging Carrie from bed on a day when she could have slept in. But Eugenia comforted herself with the knowledge that the upcoming surprise would be well worth the sacrifice of sleep.

They walked quietly to the kitchen, but instead of starting immediately on the turkey, Carrie led Eugenia to the pantry and opened the door. "I want to show you the gifts."

Eugenia stepped up and looked over Carrie's shoulder.

"This is the checkerboard I helped the boys make for Len. It took hours, but I think it turned out nicely."

Eugenia nodded. "Very nice."

Then Carrie pointed at a wooden puzzle that spelled EVAN. "Ethan painted each piece all by himself. He's so proud of the results."

"As well he should be," Eugenia said.

"Evan made those beanbags for Ethan." Carrie motioned toward a stack of imperfectly formed cloth squares. "And this is what Len was able to purchase with his restaurant money."

Eugenia studied the stacks of clothing and a few simple toys.

Carrie ran a hand lovingly over a pair of small blue jeans. "Most of the time being poor is bad, but today I'm almost grateful for our limited finances. If we had plenty of money, we would have spent a few minutes in a store picking out items for each other. But because we didn't have money, the gift-giving process involved hours of work and sacrifice."

Eugenia felt mildly alarmed. "These gifts are wonderful," she said, "but wouldn't it be nice if your boys could have more?"

Carrie shook her head and smiled. "Even if I had the ability to buy expensive toys and clothes, I wouldn't. The boys poured their hearts into these homemade gifts; how could a wooden puzzle compete with a Gameboy?"

Now Eugenia was horrified. "You're telling me that if you suddenly received a million dollars you wouldn't rush out and buy the boys better gifts for Christmas?"

"No," Carrie confirmed. "I wouldn't change our Christmas for anything—not even a million dollars!"

Eugenia stared at the little collection of gifts, thinking about the truckloads of donations headed their way that would definitely change the Carters' Christmas. She felt ill. Instead of a Christmas miracle, she'd created a Christmas nightmare.

"Are you okay, Miss Eugenia?" Carrie asked. "You look pale."

Eugenia forced a smile. "I'm fine, but could you excuse me for a second? I need to make a phone call."

"Of course," Carrie said. Then she watched in confusion as Eugenia hurried outside.

While she walked, Eugenia pulled her cell phone from her purse. She called Annabelle repeatedly but kept getting her sister's voicemail. Next she called Kate. When her young neighbor answered, Eugenia explained the dilemma and concluded with, "So, do you see that we absolutely cannot force our gifts upon the Carters?"

"I understand," Kate agreed. "But I don't know how to prevent it. The trucks are already on their way to the Carters' house. The mayor and representatives from all the local churches are riding in Whit's donated minivan. And the whole parade is being led by the Haggerty High School band."

Eugenia sat on the front porch steps, afraid that her weak knees wouldn't be able to support her. "Is Whit in one of the U-Haul trucks?"

"Yes," Kate confirmed.

"Then I'll call him and see what he can do." Eugenia hung up with Kate and desperately dialed Whit's cell number. She could already hear the distant strains of Christmas carols from the band when Whit answered.

"Hello!" he hollered to be heard above the roar of the truck's engine.

"Whit!" Eugenia cried. "We have an emergency." She repeated her succinct account of how she had badly misjudged the Carters' situation and then asked, "So, what can we do?"

"I don't know!" Whit yelled back. "I can't stop the parade! We're only a few blocks away!"

"Then we're just going to have to figure out someone else to overwhelm with Christmas cheer."

"Like who?" Whit demanded.

"Let me think." Eugenia closed her eyes and prayed for help. The Lord had never let her down before, and she was sure He'd help her now. As the sound of the Haggerty High School band playing "Holly Jolly Christmas" drew nearer, inspiration struck. "I know what to do!" she told Whit.

"What?" he asked.

"Just walk on past the hay house and go up to Dub's double-wide trailer. We'll give *him* the Christmas miracle instead."

"How are we going to explain the toys?" Whit wanted to know.

"Tell him they're for him to donate to Toys for Tots."

"What about the roofing supplies and the crew of Mormon elders?"

"Tell him a new roof for his hay house is part of his Christmas gift," Eugenia replied.

"And the minivan?"

"You'll think of something," Eugenia assured him. "Now I've got to get back inside and invite the Carters to join the parade." She ended her call, said a quick prayer of thanks, and hurried into the kitchen.

\* \* \*

By the time the Christmas miracle parade had reached the hay house, all the Carters and Eugenia were waiting along the side of the road. After everyone else had passed, they fell into step beside Kate, Mark, and the Iverson children.

They had only moved a few feet down the dirt road when Carrie put a hand to her mouth and gasped. "We don't have anything to give Uncle Dub."

"Don't worry about that," Eugenia replied. "We have plenty, believe me."

But Carrie was still frowning. Finally she leaned down and whispered something in Ethan's ear. The boy took off running into his house and returned less than a minute later clutching two Cool Whip angels.

"Why are we giving away our angels?" Evan wanted to know.

"Because that's what Christmas is about," Carrie explained. "Sharing what you have with others the way Jesus would if He were here."

Eugenia and Kate exchanged a smile as they trailed along behind the parade.

"Isn't it strange that allowing Carrie the chance to share what little she has is a better gift than giving her tons of stuff?" Kate whispered.

"It's strange all right," Eugenia agreed, and Kate laughed.

"We'd better hurry or the whole surprise will be over before we get there," Kate said.

"That might be for the best," Eugenia muttered, but she picked up her pace.

When Kate and Eugenia reached what Dub Shaw called a front yard, they saw that pandemonium had prevailed. Dogs were barking, the band was playing, and in the midst of it all stood the substitute honoree—looking confused and a little frightened.

Whit told the Boy Scouts to subdue the dogs and signaled the band into silence. Then he put an arm around Dub and, in a booming voice, explained the old man's good fortune.

"All this is for me?" Dub finally asked.

"Yes, sir!" Whit assured him. "We have furniture and decorations and food. The Mormons are going to put a new roof on your hay house, and you're the proud owner of a gently used minivan."

Dub grinned at this. "I sure am glad to hear that! I haven't had a car ever since the judge suspended my license over all those DUIs, and I'm tired of having to call a taxi to take me to my Alcoholics Anonymous meetings."

Whit frowned. "I can't turn a van over to an unlicensed driver." He surveyed the crowd until his eyes settled on Len. "Mr. Carter, could you help us out?"

Len stepped forward. "I will if I can."

"Could we impose upon you and your wife to take charge of the van until Mr. Shaw's license is restored?"

"Sure," Len agreed, and Whit tossed him the keys.

"I hate to put too big of a burden on you," Whit continued with a pained expression. "But the van will need to be driven occasionally, to keep the battery charged. And Mr. Shaw needs to be taken to his AA meetings and the grocery store—places like that."

"We'll take him," Len promised.

Whit smiled his appreciation and then said, "Okay, everybody. Let's get to work!"

The band, the dignitaries, most of the children, and the townspeople who had come just to express their good wishes were dismissed at this point, and the serious labor began. While the Mormon elders quorum roofed the hay house, the other volunteers transformed Dub's trailer into a winter wonderland. The ladies from the Haggery Baptist Church, under the direction of Polly Kirby, provided lunch.

As lunch ended, Mark found Eugenia. "Kate just called," he told her. "They've got a baby for us."

"Now?" Eugenia asked.

Mark smiled. "A little boy. We're supposed to pick him up in Macon as soon as we can get there."

"A Christmas baby," Eugenia whispered. "I guess Kate is beside herself."

"Oh, yes," Mark confirmed. "Be sure and come over this evening so we can introduce you."

"I will," Eugenia promised. "And will you let Lady out for a few minutes before you leave? I don't want her cooped up all day."

Mark nodded and then hurried off.

"Well, what do you know about that?" Eugenia whispered to herself.

\* \* \*

Finally, as the sun set, the crowd gathered in the front yard to admire their handiwork. Eugenia was amazed at what they had been able to accomplish in a few short hours. The trailer was lined with hundreds of colored lights and full of new furniture. Annabelle's silver tree sparkled through Dub's front window. Eugenia smiled as she spotted a Cool Whip angel hanging from an aluminum bough near the top.

Whit addressed the assemblage from Dub's front porch. "We'd like to thank everyone who participated in our project today. It's time for all of you to get home to your families, and Dub needs to make a last-minute trip to Albany to deliver toys for some needy children." Whit looked down at Dub. "Is there anything you'd like to say?"

Dub cleared his throat, and tears pooled in his red-rimmed, rheumy eyes. "I don't hardly know what to say," he began. "Nothing like this has ever happened to me in my whole life. I thank the Lord for good neighbors like you, and I wish you all a Merry Christmas!"

The crowd cheered, and Carrie wrapped her arms around Eugenia. "Thank you for letting us be a part of this."

Eugenia hugged the young woman and said, "It's been a good experience for all of us." Then she watched the Carters retreat into their house for their simple Christmas.

After Whit took Dub to deliver the Christmas toys, Eugenia stood at the entrance to Dub's property and thanked each volunteer as they left. From where she stood she could see the new roof on the hay house and could picture the pleasant family gathering within. Ethan would present his homemade puzzle to Evan. Evan would give the beanbags to his brother. And without the distraction of expensive store-bought toys, both boys would be pleased with their gifts.

Finally only Annabelle remained. "Will you give me a ride home?" she asked Eugenia. "I don't think I can walk all the way back to town."

"Sure," Eugenia agreed.

During the drive, Eugenia braced herself, expecting Annabelle to gloat over the failure of Eugenia's Christmas miracle, but Annabelle was surprisingly kind. They talked a little about Christmases past, unreasonable expectations, and the advantages of being humble.

Finally Eugenia said, "I'm sorry today was such a disaster."

Annabelle smiled. "You meant well."

"I wanted to give the Carters the best Christmas ever," Eugenia explained. "But I realized too late that they didn't need me for that."

"You didn't accomplish what you set out to do," Annabelle said, "but I don't think we can consider the day a total loss. You had the whole town working together, you gave the Carters a chance to contribute, and Dub will never be the same."

Eugenia laughed. "That's all true!"

Annabelle reached over and patted her sister's hand. "Merry Christmas, Eugenia."

Eugenia blinked back happy, exhausted tears. "Merry Christmas to you, too."

\* \* \*

Eugenia dropped Annabelle off at the Family Life center where her car was parked. Then she drove toward home, anxious to see if the Iversons were back with their foster baby. She turned the corner onto Maple Street, and all thoughts of the Iversons disappeared when she saw Whit's car parked at the curb in front of her house.

He met her on the front sidewalk.

"Did you get the toys delivered?" she asked him.

"We did."

Eugenia smiled. "I can't thank you enough for all you did today."

"Yes you can," he corrected her. "You can make good on that date you owe me."

"Unfortunately for you, all the restaurants close early on Christmas Eve," she said.

"That's just as well since we're not really dressed to go out. I guess I'll be forced to fix you dinner at my place."

"No point in going to a lot of trouble," she said. "We'll just heat up some chicken soup here." She glanced over at the Iversons' house. "That is, after I go next door and see Kate and Mark's new foster baby."

Whit's eyes followed hers. "It's kind of late," he mentioned. "Kate and Mark are probably tucking their kids into bed, preparing for Santa to come."

"Yes," she agreed wistfully.

"It would be a shame to bother them." He put a hand on her elbow and propelled her gently toward her front door. "Maybe you could meet the new baby tomorrow."

She raised an eyebrow. "Why are you suddenly so interested in protecting the Iversons' family time?"

He laughed. "It's been a long day, and I'm hungry."

Eugenia couldn't argue with that. "It has been a long day, but a good one. I've learned that you can't give someone the perfect Christmas. Unless the true spirit of Christmas is in their hearts, it won't happen no matter how many gifts they receive."

Whit nodded. "That's a good lesson to learn. And who said you can't teach an old dog new tricks?"

"Whit Owens, did you just call me an old dog?"

"Heavens no!" Whit said, obviously startled by the accusation.

While she had him off balance, Eugenia decided to shock him more. So she leaned over and gave him a big Christmas kiss, right on the lips.

"How's that for an old trick?" she teased. Then she walked into the house, confident that he would follow.

# A Port in the Storm
## by Michele Ashman Bell

*Day 1*

"Sophie, you can't spend Christmas alone; I won't let you," Amanda Rogers said. "Come to San Francisco with us. My folks have plenty of room. They would love to have you join us."

"I appreciate the offer, I really do," Sophie said as she shifted her cell phone to the other ear and guided her silver Acura along the winding mountain road toward the Pacific coast, "but you know I don't do the whole Christmas thing. I just want to be alone. Really, it's better this way."

"You're my best friend. It breaks my heart to think of you alone."

"Then don't think about me. I'm fine. You and Frank have a wonderful time with your family." Sophie noticed a sign indicating that she was close to

Cannon Beach. She had reservations at a wonderful bed-and-breakfast there and had a trunk full of books she'd been saving to read over the holidays. Amanda didn't need to worry about her.

"Okay," Amanda said dejectedly. "But promise me you'll call if you change your mind."

"I promise."

"And try to have a Merry Christmas."

"Uh, thanks. You too," Sophie answered abruptly, not wanting to hear any more Christmas cheer.

Sophie ended the call and turned on her low beams. The drive from Portland wasn't long, but a storm was brewing, so she had to negotiate the roads carefully. She hadn't anticipated having to drive in bad weather, something that made her very, very anxious. She was all too ready to check into her room, soak in a hot tub, and relax.

The owners of the Cape House Bed-and-Breakfast were expecting Sophie to arrive late. They'd said they would have dinner and a warm fire waiting for her. She'd found Cape House on the Internet and was immediately drawn to the castle-like structure. She couldn't explain it, but she felt a connection, probably because it looked like the perfect place to escape—something she'd done every year at this time for the last three years.

Memories tried to surface, but she quickly pushed them down and focused on the winding road. This was a vacation—from work, from the city, and from the past. All she wanted was a view of the ocean, some famous Oregon coast clam chowder, and a good book.

To break the silence she turned on the radio, but as she scanned the stations, all she got were Christmas carols. She turned the radio off, preferring the silence.

Heading a few miles south of Cannon Beach, Sophie followed the roads indicated on the map that led to Cape House. As she neared the main structure, lit up by sparkling Christmas lights and festive wreaths, Sophie was caught up in the charm of it all.

Pulling into a parking stall, she slid the car into park and rested her head back on the seat for a moment. Wind and scattered drops of rain beat against her car. The storm was about to let loose. She'd made it just in time.

Popping the trunk, Sophie climbed out of the car and reached for her suitcase and garment bag only to receive a stern, "Hold it right there, young lady. I'll get that!"

She turned to see an elderly man toddling her way. His rotund belly and waddling walk were immediately endearing.

"Welcome to Cape House," he said.

"Thank you. It looks like I got here just in time," she said over the noise of the impending storm.

"We were getting a little worried. The missus was glad to see your car pull into the driveway. Noreen has a pot of chowder on the stove for you."

"That's just what I wanted to hear. My mouth's been watering since Portland."

"You scoot on inside. I'll bring in your bags." He shooed her with his hand.

Sophie walked up the four stairs to the landing and paused. A giant swag of twisted twigs and pine boughs laced with lights hung over the massive wooden door. Some sort of magic emanated from the Bavarian-style structure.

The door creaked open, and she stepped inside, greeted by the warm glow of the fireplace at the opposite end of the room and the tantalizing aroma of freshly baked bread and clam chowder.

She loved the wooden beamed ceiling, the stone tiled floors, the paneled walls, and the massive fireplace in the main sitting room. In the corner stood an enormous twelve-foot Christmas tree, trimmed in gold and burgundy ornaments along with hundreds of lights. The mantel was aglow with burning candles and pine boughs.

Placed generously around the room was a collection of nutcrackers and Nativity scenes. "It's Beginning to Look a Lot Like Christmas" played softly in the background.

Following her nose through the dining room and into the kitchen, Sophie found Noreen at the stove stirring a pot of chowder. The woman turned when she heard Sophie's heels clicking against the stone floor.

"Goodness gracious!" she exclaimed, stepping away from the stove. "Look who's here!" Noreen was about the same height as Sophie, which made her a good four inches taller than her husband. She was an attractive woman with honey-blond hair, bright blue eyes, and a warm smile.

Sophie expected a handshake but got a hug instead.

"You must be tired and famished from your drive. I have a place set for you in the dining room. Or if you'd rather not eat in there all alone, you're welcome to eat here in the kitchen."

Sophie surprised herself when she said, "I think I'd like to eat in here if you don't mind."

"Of course, dear. Have a seat at the table there, and I'll dish you up some chowder. I've got some rolls fresh out of the oven too."

"I smelled them when I came in. They made my mouth water."

Noreen smiled proudly.

"Have the other guests eaten?" Sophie asked as she sat at the small kitchen table.

"Yes. Several of them are gone for the evening, and we also have two older couples staying with us. They retire quite early, though."

Noreen filled a bowl and placed it in front of Sophie along with a giant steaming hot roll on a plate and homemade raspberry jam.

Sophie tasted a small spoonful of chowder then shut her eyes and sighed. "That was worth the drive right there."

Noreen chuckled. "Remind me to send some food home with you when you leave. You look like you could use some fattening up."

"I don't really like to cook just for one," Sophie told her, breaking off a piece of the fluffy dinner roll and smearing jam on it.

Outside, the bitter wind howled.

"So how long have you been here at Cape House?" Sophie asked between bites of chowder.

"Goodness, let me think. We came here in ninety-seven, after Bert retired. He'd been working in Portland at the Longview Lumber Company, just like his father. We'd always wanted a place on the coast, and when we found out that Cape House was for sale, we realized it was the perfect place to retire."

"Where do your children live?" Sophie asked.

"We were never able to have any children," Noreen told her sadly. "It's been a struggle for us, but I don't suppose any of us get through life without a few struggles, do we?"

Sophie agreed. Life for her seemed as though it

were one big struggle. She'd given up trying to figure out the purpose of trials.

Bert entered the kitchen, rubbing his hands together to warm them.

"I put your bags in your room," he told Sophie. "We put you in the Tower Room. It has the best view of the ocean."

"It's my favorite room," Noreen told her. "When you requested a bathtub instead of a shower, I knew exactly which room to give you."

A yawn snuck up on Sophie, and she covered her mouth with her hand.

"Our guest is exhausted, Bert," Noreen said. "Why don't you take her up to her room to get settled. I'll tidy up the kitchen and then come and check on you. If you need anything, just buzz me from your room."

Sophie appreciated their attentiveness and warmth. She felt very welcome and appreciated that they didn't pry.

The room was even more spectacular than the picture on the website. It had a lovely sitting area in the tower, surrounded by a ring of windows. The oval tub was tucked away in an alcove, leaving a large space for the queen-sized bed with a Louis XIV carved wood head- and foot-board and a thick down comforter. A private fireplace with cozy chairs and a French armoire of fruitwood completed the furnishings.

"Breakfast is anytime between seven and ten in the morning," Bert told her. "After you get settled, you can come down for some cookies, Noreen bakes some every night for our guests."

"Thank you," Sophie said. "You've both been so wonderful."

"We just want to make you feel at home."

Bert closed the door behind him and the room grew silent, except for the wind and rain beating at the windows. She shuddered, then went to the tub and turned on the hot water. This place was exactly what she needed.

* * *

## Day 2

The next morning when Sophie awoke, sunlight flooded the room. She had to squint against its brightness but stayed in bed, snuggled in the warmth of the fluffy down comforter.

The aroma of cinnamon filled the air and made Sophie's mouth water. Generally not a breakfast person, she realized she was hungry.

*Must be the sea air,* Sophie thought.

Pulling on her thick fleece robe, she wandered to the sitting area and looked out the window to the coastline below. Stray branches and debris were strewn about the shoreline and the Cape House parking lot. The storm from the night before had really done some damage. Movement out of the corner of Sophie's eye caught her attention. Bert was gathering the broken tree limbs and twigs cluttering the yard and driveway.

Changing into jeans and a sweater, Sophie descended the stairs just as the last set of guests left the dining room.

"Am I too late?" she asked Noreen, who was clearing the table.

"Heavens no!" Noreen exclaimed. "I have plenty. How did you sleep, dear?"

"I was afraid the wind would keep me up all night, but I slept right through it."

"That was quite a storm we had. Made a big mess outside, especially down on the beach."

After a delicious breakfast of eggs, bacon, and freshly baked cinnamon rolls, Sophie pulled on her winter coat, gloves, and hat and went outside the mansion to get some fresh air.

A light breeze blew, making the mid-thirty-degree temperature feel a little cooler, but the sun felt warm on her face, and the air was fresh and invigorating.

Following the driveway, she walked along the side of the road, admiring the majestic pines and marveling at the deep blue sky. It was a glorious day.

Several painted boards nailed to a post indicated that hiking trails were one direction and the beach was another.

Sophie found herself taking the beach path to a flight of wooden stairs leading to the shoreline below.

The call of gulls overhead and the crash of waves on the sand filled the air, crowding out her thoughts. The power and expanse of the ocean made her feel small in comparison, but there was also a sense of freedom and appreciation for the beauty surrounding her.

In the distance a dog barked and a couple strolled hand in hand. Sophie diverted her eyes and turned her attention to the frothy waves crashing to the shore. Love had escaped her in life. She'd dated a lot, but none of the men she dated seemed like marriage material. Now she was beginning to wonder if there was something wrong with her.

Stepping over flotsam washed ashore by the storm, she continued to walk until she came to a rocky outcropping that prevented her from going further.

Just as she was about to turn around, a reflection partially hidden by seaweed caught her eye. She bent forward to get a closer look, clearing the seaweed away with her hand, and discovered an old green bottle.

Amazed that it hadn't broken in its journey to the shore, she reached for the bottle and lifted it up to take a closer look. She was surprised to see a piece of paper rolled up inside.

"Whoa," she said upon closer inspection, wondering if it was what she thought it was. The paper looked like it had been written on. A message.

Keeping a firm grip on the bottle, she cut her walk short and decided to go back to her room and see what was inside the bottle.

As she entered Cape House, she put the bottle under her jacket to keep it out of sight. She didn't want to show anyone until she knew what she'd found.

Once in her room, she placed the sand-encrusted bottle on a towel and stared at it for a moment, her imagination going every direction.

What could the note possibly say? Who could have written it?

There was only one way to find out, but when she tried to unscrew the lid, she realized it was a hopeless effort. She knew she could break the bottle, but something inside her told her to save that for a last resort.

Maybe if she had some pliers or something that would help her get a good grip on the lid.

She had no choice but to ask Bert for help.

Several guests were relaxing in front of the fire, sipping hot wassail and listening to Christmas carols playing in the background. Sophie nodded to the guests without stopping to be bothered by the music. Leaving the sitting room, she continued to look for Bert.

Instead, she found Noreen, who was in the kitchen working on lunch.

"Hello, deary. How was your walk?" Noreen asked.

"Fascinating," Sophie responded. "I found something interesting on the beach."

Noreen finished cutting chicken chunks into a bowl and began mixing the ingredients together for chicken salad croissants. "You'd be surprised what washes up on our beaches, especially after a hefty storm like we had last night. Bert is always bringing home some crazy object he's found down there. Why, one day he brought home a pair of Nike shoes. He actually found both shoes, same size and everything. Later we found out that a cargo ship carrying a whole load of Nike shoes had sunk. We had shoes washing up on shore for weeks!"

"I didn't find any shoes," Sophie said, "but I found this." She held up the bottle for Noreen to see.

Noreen glanced over her shoulder. "An old bottle. That's interesting," she said with a bit of sarcasm.

Sophie smiled. She liked this woman.

"There's a message inside."

Noreen stopped stirring and looked directly at Sophie.

"A message? Are you sure?"

"Well, there's a rolled up piece of paper inside and there are words written on it. But I can't get the lid off to read it."

Noreen wiped her hands on a dishtowel and joined Sophie at the table. "May I?" she asked, nodding at the bottle.

"Of course," Sophie answered.

Noreen studied the bottle, turning it over in her hands and peering closely to try to make out any of the words on the paper. "This thing looks like it's been bobbing around in the water for years. No wonder the lid's fused on there so tightly. The saltwater has corroded it."

"I'd like to try to get the lid off without breaking it," Sophie said.

"Bert loves stuff like this. I bet he could get the lid off." Noreen put the bottle down on the table, then went to open the back door. She called for her husband several times before coming back inside. "Still a bit nippy out there. We won't have a white Christmas, but it's certainly going to be a cold one."

Sophie didn't mind if there wasn't snow for Christmas. For her, it would be just another day, which she planned on spending curled up in her room getting lost in a book.

Outside the door, Sophie heard the stomp of boots on the steps and Bert grumbling.

He burst inside and continued his complaints. "Blasted furnace is acting up again. Don't think I can salvage it this time. I'd better put a call in to Charlie before the holiday. Don't want to freeze our guests for Christmas. What did you need? It's not lunchtime yet, is it? I was busy!"

"Now, Bert, not in front of our guest," Noreen said. "Look, Sophie here has found something you might be interested in, and she needs your help."

Bert pulled off his gloves and hat and dropped them on the counter, then pulled out a chair and sat down at the table, picking up the bottle.

"Well, I'll be. Where'd you find this?" he asked.

"On the beach," Sophie said. "Near the point. I can't get the lid off."

He examined the bottle closely then attempted to twist off the lid, with no luck. "That lid is on there good."

"I don't want to break it."

He nodded. "Let's see what we can do."

Bert opened a drawer in the kitchen, pulled out a few tools, and brought them back to the table.

He tried tapping and twisting and pulling, but the lid didn't budge.

"How about a little oil, to lubricate the lid?" Noreen offered.

"It's worth a shot," he said, handing the bottle to her.

Noreen put some drops of lubricant around the edge of the lid and allowed it to seep in, then handed the bottle to her husband.

"I've found pretty much everything imaginable on that beach out there," Bert said, "but I've never found a bottle with a message inside."

When he was satisfied that the oil had worked some magic, Bert tried to twist off the lid one more time. "Dad-blast-it!"

"Bert!"

"Well, the confounded thing won't come off."

"I guess we'll have to break it," Sophie said. "The most interesting thing is the note, anyway."

Noreen looked at the bottle with new appreciation. "How in the world can something as fragile as glass be so strong?"

"A well-sealed bottle is one of the world's most seaworthy objects," Bert explained. "It can survive a hurricane that would sink a great ship. Glass lasts forever. I've heard stories of 250-year-old bottles being found in sunken ships in perfect condition. I hate to break her," Bert said, picking up the bottle, "but it's the only way to get what's inside."

Bert wrapped the bottle in a dish towel and, taking the hammer in his other hand, gave the bottle a giant whack. The sturdy glass shattered in the towel.

Bert's face lit up, showing his excitement that mirrored Sophie's own. Taking the towel from Bert and placing it on the table, Sophie carefully unwrapped it to reveal the rolled-up note lying in a pile of glass.

Gently she lifted the note from the mess. Sun damage and age had made the paper crisp, and she feared it would crumble in her fingers. With slow, careful movements she unrolled the paper and laid it flat on the table. The writing had faded and was difficult to see, but the words were still legible.

*Dearest Viola,*

*The Devil's Wind is churning up the water something fierce. I know you may never get this message, but I have to write down how I feel.*

*How I wish I could hold you and tell you how sorry I am for the way we said good-bye. I would give anything to take back everything I said. Please, darling, forgive me. I love you. And I will love our child with all of my heart.*

*Tell your father that this is my last run. As soon as I get home, I'll go to work for him at Tillamook Lumber. I want to be home with you and our child, not gone for weeks at a time risking my life crab fishing.*

*I'll be home in time for Christmas, and we can talk then and plan our life together. Please forgive me.*

*I love you,*

*Ernest*

"Well, imagine that," Bert said. "He probably worked for a commercial fishing company. Dungeness crab season begins in December. Dangerous job, commercial fishing. Especially if they head up into the Alaskan waters. You get waves six meters high, with snow, hail, and ice storms in the winter. A fisherman falls overboard and within minutes hypothermia sets in. Charlie, our furnace guy, was a fisherman for a while, but he finally gave it up because it was so dangerous. Good money, though. That's why most men are willing to take the risk."

Noreen wiped tears from her eyes with the corner of her apron. "I wonder what happened."

"I hope he made it home," Sophie said. "I wonder what the Devil's Wind is."

"It's a hurricane force wind that hits during the winter. Been known to capsize many a fishing boat. These men risk their lives when they go out there in those waters during the winter."

They stared at the letter for several seconds, digesting this information and what it meant for Ernest and his message.

"I wonder how long ago he wrote this," Sophie said.

"I wonder if he and Viola worked things out," Noreen added.

"You know, there is a way to find out all the answers to these questions," Bert said.

Noreen and Sophie looked at him.

"Tillamook Lumber's not too far from here. We have names, and we have a place of employment. Can't be that hard. I'm sure Ernest will be amazed his message finally washed up on shore."

"If, in fact, he made it home." Noreen voiced Sophie's fear.

"If he didn't, all the more reason we should track down Viola."

Sophie agreed. How she wished she had a message like this to help bring closure in her own life.

"Sophie, you feel like driving to Tillamook this afternoon?" Noreen asked.

"Can you get away?" she replied, glancing first at Noreen and then at Bert.

"I'll get Charlie over here to work on the furnace. He can keep an eye on the place while we're gone. One of Noreen's home-cooked meals and he'll do pretty much anything we ask."

"Just let me get lunch on the table, and then we can go."

"Can I help?" Sophie offered, knowing that staying busy would be the best way to kill time until they left.

"Are you sure, dear? You don't have to."

"I'd rather stay busy."

Noreen patted her hand. "I'm anxious to meet Ernest and Viola, too." She got to her feet. "I'd love your help."

The two women worked side by side, making sandwiches and dishing up bowls of hot vegetable soup.

While the guests ate their fill in the dining room, Noreen and Sophie grabbed a quick bite in the kitchen.

"I thought I was going to spend my vacation up in my room reading," Sophie said. "Who knew I'd find a message in a bottle and try to solve a mystery?"

"Isn't that just the way life is? Filled with unexpected surprises. Just gotta keep moving. Gotta keep the faith."

Sophie didn't answer. She didn't know what say. She'd lost her faith.

"Just like that bottle that bobbed around in the ocean for who knows how long, then finally washed up on shore. Without faith, you'll float around aimlessly until you finally wash up on shore."

*The Spirit of Christmas: Stories of the Season*

Without admitting it, Sophie knew Noreen was right. She felt exactly like that—a bottle floating around aimlessly. She'd been raised LDS and had always gone to church with her family and done all the things she was expected to do. But she supposed that she just went through the motions without ever gaining a real testimony of her own. And then, when the accident happened, she had nothing to fall back on. It was one thing knowing about the plan of salvation; it was another thing actually believing it.

Bert clambered through the back door into the kitchen in his work boots and winter coat. "Charlie's here. He thinks he can repair the furnace with an old rebuilt part. You girls about ready?"

Noreen and Sophie looked at each other with amusement. They'd had the table cleared and the dishes done for half an hour as they patiently waited for Bert.

"We're ready, dear," Noreen told him.

"Well, grab your coats then. We're off to solve a mystery."

\* \* \*

Tillamook wasn't that far away, but the drive seemed to stretch on for eternity. Bert had the radio tuned to a station playing Christmas carols. He whistled along with a peppy rendition of "Let it Snow." The message, safely stored in a clear sheet protector, sat on Sophie's lap where she read and reread the contents several times. Viola and Ernest seemed to become more and more real in her imagination as she mulled over questions in her mind. What had been said on that final parting that had upset Ernest so much? Had learning about Viola having a child been upsetting to him? Why? Had he made it safely back to shore and into the arms of Viola, his love?

Gaily decorated street lamps and store windows painted with holiday scenes greeted them as they drove into the picturesque town.

"I say we go directly to the lumberyard and find out anything we can about Ernest," Bert suggested. "From the way he worded his message, it sounds like Viola's father might have owned the place at one time."

"Good idea," Noreen said, checking with Sophie for a confirming nod. The lumberyard was their only definite clue.

"If I remember right, the lumber yard is on the other side of town," Bert said.

"I wrote down the address, just in case," Noreen replied, pulling a piece of Cape House stationery out of her coat pocket. "It should be just down the street here. This is exciting, isn't it?" Noreen said, glancing back at Sophie. "I can't help but wonder what kind of impact this information will have on Viola."

"I hope Ernest came home and they lived happily ever after," Sophie replied.

"There it is!" Bert announced as he turned off the main street onto a side road. But his enthusiasm quickly vanished as he pulled the car up to the locked front gate with a large CLOSED sign plastered across it.

"Oh, dear," Noreen said. "I wonder when that happened."

"Blasted chain stores! Between Lowe's and Home Depot, these poor independent fellas don't stand a chance," Bert exclaimed.

"There's a car over by the side of the building," Sophie noticed. "Maybe someone is in there and can give us some information."

"Worth a try," Bert grumbled.

They climbed out of the car and walked over to a doorway by the side of the gate. A cold wind was blowing, and Sophie pulled her coat close around her, wishing she'd worn a hat and gloves.

"Goodness," Noreen said, shoving her hands into her pockets to keep them warm. "Quite a nip in the air."

Bert tried the door, but it was locked. He banged on it loudly.

They waited, hoping someone would answer, but there didn't seem to be anyone around.

"Guess we could go to the city offices and see what they know," Bert suggested.

Sophie and Noreen nodded and walked back to the car. Just as they were getting in, a voice called from behind the locked fence. "Can I help you folks?"

A face peered at them through the chain links.

"Hello," Bert responded. "We're looking for anyone who might have some information about a previous owner of the lumberyard."

"Oh? What's this regarding?"

"Well, we've got quite an interesting story. Not sure how to explain it."

"I'm not in a position to listen," the man said in a hurry. "I'm late for an important meeting."

"Not a problem," Bert said, "We'll let you be on your way then."

Bert climbed into the car.

"Wait," Noreen called to the man. She rushed over to the fence and handed him the paper from her coat pocket. "Our phone number is on there. If you know of someone who would be willing to talk, we have some information that might be of interest to them." The man took the paper but didn't respond.

Noreen got back in the car and pulled the door shut behind her.

"What a grump!" she exclaimed.

"We caught him at a bad time, I guess," Sophie said, wishing the man could have been a little more helpful.

"Forget about him," Bert said. "The city office building will have something on record."

But Bert was wrong. No one at the city office could locate the records they needed. The woman at the information desk promised to ask around and see if anyone could remember or knew where to locate the records. She said she would call if she had any luck, but Sophie doubted she would try very hard.

Disappointed, Sophie got back in the car.

"Don't despair, deary," Noreen told her. "Something will turn up. We'll give them a couple of days, then we'll call them to see if someone has remembered something."

Sophie gave her an appreciative smile, but inside she lost hope that they would find Viola or Ernest.

That evening Sophie stayed holed up in her room, coming downstairs only long enough to have a bite of dinner. Most of the guests had checked out and were headed back home to spend Christmas with family and loved ones. As far as she knew, Sophie would be the only guest there over the holiday, just two days away.

\* \* \*

*Day 3*

The next day, Sophie drove to Tillamook to do a little shopping. Even though she didn't plan on participating in any festivities for the holidays, she did feel a need to buy something for Bert and Noreen. They'd been so kind and caring, and she wanted them to know how much she appreciated them. Not to mention that she wasn't as keen on the idea of sitting in her room all day reading as she thought she would be. She'd never been one to sit around and do nothing—why had she thought she would suddenly become that way overnight for her vacation?

After a quick drive to Tillamook, Sophie found a couple of nice shops where she hoped she would find some suitable gifts for Bert and Noreen.

She'd noticed that Bert's coat was quite worn and frayed. She found him a nice Pendleton wool jacket that looked like something he would enjoy. For Noreen, she found pair of leather gloves and a new black leather handbag. Noreen's bag looked like it had seen better days, and what woman didn't enjoy a new purse?

As she took her purchases to the register, she stopped at a display of Christmas sweets, eyeing a box of chocolates to add to her gifts.

"Have you ever tried one of those chocolates?" a voice said.

Sophie turned to find a nice-looking man approximately her age standing beside her. His name tag read JACK MCRAE.

"No. They look good though."

"I guarantee they're the best chocolates you'll ever taste. Made right here in town." He pulled a box from behind the display. "Try one. I recommend the mint truffle; it's our most popular."

Sophie lifted one from the box and took a bite, letting the creamy goodness melt in her mouth. "Oh," she said, closing her eyes. "That is good." She swallowed. "I'd better buy two boxes."

The man chuckled and picked up another box. "Will that be all?"

She thought about her friends and coworkers. They were always bringing treats in to the office. She knew the truffles would be a big hit with them.

"Why don't you get me five more boxes," she said.

"Five?" His eyes opened wide.

Now Sophie laughed. "They're not all for me."

He picked up the requested amount of boxes and escorted her to the checkout stand.

"Are you just in town for the holidays?" he asked, starting to ring up her purchases.

"Uh, yes," she said.

"Where are you from?" he asked, putting the items in bags for her.

"Portland," she answered, pulling her credit card out of her wallet.

"Would you like gift boxes for these?" he offered.

"Yes! Thank you. I forgot I don't have anything to wrap the gifts in."

He put several gift boxes, tissue paper, and ribbon in another sack.

Sophie handed him her card.

"Are you enjoying your stay?"

"Yes. It's a much slower pace here than in Portland. That's nice."

"I worked in Portland for quite a while," he said. "I had to move back a few years ago. I don't really miss the hectic pace of the city, although there's a lot more to do there than there is here. I miss all the sporting events and going to plays."

"It's not that far of a drive from here."

"No, it's not. I have a hard time getting away, though. There is a concert here in town tonight. Tillamook has an exceptional choir. You should come." His gaze held hers for a moment.

Sophie blinked and quickly looked down at the receipt she needed to sign. "I'm not sure what I have planned yet for this evening, but I'll keep that in mind." She scrawled her signature on the paper and handed it back to him.

He accepted it with a warm smile. She liked how lively his eyes were, how sincere his expression was.

*The Spirit of Christmas: Stories of the Season*

After the false politeness of so many men in the city, Sophie appreciated how genuine this man seemed.

"I hope you'll come back and see us again before you leave town," he said, handing her bags to her. "I'm going to have a great after-Christmas sale."

"The chocolate?"

"I'll give you the volume discount," he told her.

She laughed, surprised at how comfortable she felt with him.

Again, their gazes locked. Then the door to the store opened and several customers walked inside, giving him holiday greetings.

Deciding that she indeed would come and pay one last visit before she left to go back home, she thanked him for his help and said good-bye.

"Merry Christmas, Sophie," he said, reading her name off her credit card receipt.

Hearing him say her name caught her off guard for a moment. "Same to you, Jack."

He flashed his incredible smile at her again, then turned when one of the new customers asked him a question.

Sophie shifted the bags in her hand so she could open the front door. She glanced back quickly before she left, and she saw Jack looking at her.

He nodded at her and smiled once again.

She left feeling a warmth inside she hadn't felt for many years.

\* \* \*

*Day 4*

As the only guest left at Cape House, Sophie had the place to herself the next day. Bert was outside working around the yard, and Noreen was busy in the kitchen making pies for Christmas day. Noreen told Sophie that they usually had six to eight people over for dinner on Christmas day, mostly friends from town or guests who happened to be staying with them through the holiday.

With no risk of being bothered by other guests, Sophie brought her book downstairs and curled up in a wingback chair by the fire instead of staying in her room.

Between the spicy, sweet smells coming from the kitchen and the soft Christmas music playing through the house, Sophie found herself thinking of Christmases past and how much she'd loved the whole Christmas season as a child.

She closed her eyes and allowed herself to remember the special Christmas memories with her family. It usually began with the tree.

The day after Thanksgiving every year, Sophie would beg her mother to put up the Christmas tree. It was an annual event, and they would work for hours putting on dozens of strands of lights. Her mother loved lights. Sophie was the official light tester, thoroughly testing each strand before putting it on the tree. Nothing irked her mother more than having a strand of lights go out.

Once the tree was done, Sophie and her brother Ben would spend hours cutting paper snowflakes and helping their mother frost sugar cookies to take around to the neighbors. Her mother's recipe had been handed down from Sophie's great-grandmother, and it made the best sugar cookies Sophie had ever tasted.

Her father would come in from shoveling snow, which they always received an abundance of in Southern Idaho, and they would drink hot chocolate together and eat the sugar cookies reserved for the family. Then they would snuggle by the fire and read Christmas stories.

With her eyes shut and the warmth of the fire and the comfy chair, Sophie soon dozed off while daydreaming in her memories. She wasn't sure how long she slept before she was awakened by a male voice.

"Excuse me, miss; I'm looking for the owner."

Sophie stifled a yawn. "I think Noreen is in the kitchen," she said as she forced her eyes open.

She looked up at the man who spoke to her and recognized him immediately. "Jack!" she exclaimed. "What a surprise."

His face registered confusion. "I'm sorry, do we know each . . ." He looked at her more closely. "Sophie? How are you? Are you a guest here?"

"I am," she said. "And you're looking for the owner?" She reached up and smoothed her hair.

"Yes. I'm sorry I disturbed your nap."

She waved away his worry. "Not at all. I just got way too comfy."

"Can't say I blame you. This is a wonderful place. Very cozy. I've never been here before."

"What brings you here now, if I may ask?"

"Well," he reached into his shirt pocket and pulled out a piece of paper, "this." He showed her a sheet of Cape House stationery. "I think they came by the lumberyard the other day."

"The lumberyard?" she asked excitedly.

"Yes. I had to stop by and check on things, but I was running late for an important appointment and I couldn't really talk to them. I felt bad about it afterward. I decided to come by and see what they needed."

So *he* was the guy behind the fence that didn't have time to help them. What a stroke of genius for Noreen to have given him the paper with the Cape House address on it.

Sophie got up from her chair.

"Well, Noreen should be in the kitchen making dinner. Here, I'll show you." She led the way to the kitchen where Noreen was busy mixing up a batch of crab cakes.

"Noreen, you have a visitor," Sophie said

Noreen stopped mixing the ingredients and turned to see Jack standing beside Sophie. She smiled and quickly wiped her hand on a towel before she extended it to Jack, introducing herself.

Sophie introduced Jack. "Noreen, Jack was the man at the lumberyard."

The older woman's mouth dropped open.

"In fact," Sophie continued, "I bumped into Jack in town yesterday when I went shopping. I didn't know who he was then."

Jack smiled at Noreen.

"Here," Noreen motioned to a chair at the table, "please sit down. Can I get you something to drink? Are you hungry? I have pumpkin pie."

"You should try it," Sophie encouraged. "It's the best I've ever tasted."

"If it's not too much trouble," Jack said, "I'd love some."

"Sophie, would you like some?"

"None for me, thanks. I've eaten so much of your pie already, I'm going to have to buy a bigger car to drive home in."

Noreen chuckled as she busied herself getting Jack a slice of pie with a light dollop of whipped cream on top. "There you go."

"That looks delicious," he said. He tested the point of the piece of pie. "Mmm, it tastes delicious, too."

Noreen beamed with pride. "I'm glad you like it. I guess you're wondering why we came by the lumberyard, seeing how it's closed and all. How are you connected to the lumberyard?" Noreen asked as she took a seat at the table with Sophie and Jack.

"Well, my grandfather owned the lumberyard, but about twenty years ago, when I was ten, he had a stroke. My mother took over the business and ran it for him. He was still able to work a few days a week, but he was never the same after that. He taught my mother everything she needed to know and she took over, until—"

"Until what?" Sophie couldn't help asking.

"She had a stroke two years ago at the age of fifty-five. Apparently there's a gene for early strokes in our family. She hasn't fully recovered. In fact," he looked down at the plate of pie in front of him, "she's at a care center right now. The doctors don't think she'll ever recover."

"I'm so terribly sorry," Noreen said.

Sophie echoed Noreen's words.

"Thank you. She's an amazing woman. Very strong. She's had a very hard life, though. Anyway, after the stroke, she wasn't there to keep the business going. I moved home from Portland, where I'd been working, and tried to step in, but the lumber business wasn't going well. It was hard to compete with the big chains. We finally closed the doors about six months ago."

"Jack, what's your mother's name?" Sophie asked.

"Her name? It's Viola, Viola McCrae."

Noreen and Sophie looked at each other. Sophie felt an overwhelming wave of emotion come over her and noticed that Noreen was also getting teary-eyed.

Jack turned his head slightly, one brow raised.

"Is your mother still able to communicate?" Noreen asked, clearing her throat.

"Oh, yes. Her mind is still sharp and clear most of the time, which makes it so hard for her. She's only fifty-seven. Some days she seems a lot like her old self. But some days she seems like a shell. It's hard to see her like this."

Sophie's heart ached for Jack and his mother.

Jack's brow furrowed with confusion. "I'm sorry, but I don't understand. Do you know my mother?"

"Sophie," Noreen said, "why don't you explain to this young man what's going on."

Sophie cleared her throat, not sure where to begin. "Jack," she said, "was your mother ever married?"

"Briefly. To my father."

"Was his name Ernest?"

His eyes narrowed. "Yes." He looked at Noreen, then back at Sophie.

"I know this is going to sound crazy, but the other day after that big storm, I went for a walk on the beach. I found a bottle, and inside the bottle I found . . ." Noreen handed Sophie the note in the sheet protector, "this." She handed the noted to him.

"What is it?" he asked without looking at it.

"Read it," she told him.

Jack studied the faint writing, reading the words scrawled on the paper. A moment later his hand, holding the paper, dropped to his lap. He shook his head, which was still bent. "I don't believe this," he whispered.

"I *still* can't believe it," Sophie said. "We had to break the bottle to get the message out. I have to ask, did Ernest come home?"

He shook his head slowly, then he looked up. "She has never—" He shut his eyes and pursed his lips for a moment. Then he cleared his throat and attempted to speak again. "She has never gotten over losing him. Never dated, never considered marrying again." He looked down at the note. "She never got to tell him good-bye.

*The Spirit of Christmas: Stories of the Season*

They'd had a big fight. She still struggles with good-byes." He sat silent for a moment. "Now I know why."

"He loved her. And he loved you," Noreen said.

"Sounds like he would've done anything to get back home," Sophie said.

Jack nodded. Then he looked at the note in his hand again. "I just can't believe this. Mom is never going to believe it. This will mean the whole world to her."

"She'll finally get to know," Sophie said, painfully aware of the unanswered questions in her own life.

Jack looked at her, his expression filled with gratitude. "If I could give her one thing before she passes away, it would be to let her know that my father did love her and that he wanted to be with us, to be a family. She would finally have peace. Thank you," he said. "You made this possible."

Sophie shrugged. "I just happened to be in the right place at the right time."

"Thank heavens you were." He cleared his throat and lifted the paper. "I have to go. I have to tell her."

He got up from his chair and looked around for his coat, which was draped over the chair back. Slipping his arms into the sleeves, he zipped it up and stopped, looking directly at Sophie. "I want you to come with me. Would you, please?"

"Oh, no." She shook her head. "I don't want to intrude."

"It would mean a lot to her, for you to tell her how you found the bottle. Please."

Sophie looked at Noreen, who just smiled at her.

"You're sure? I'm a complete stranger," Sophie said.

"I'm sure."

Sophie wasn't sure what she was getting herself in to, but she didn't have the heart to resist Jack's heartfelt request.

"Drive safely," Noreen said. "And give our best to your mother. We'll say a little prayer for her."

"Thank you," Jack said. "Thank you for everything."

\* \* \*

The ride to the care center was quiet but not awkward, which was amazing to Sophie. Except for her interaction with business associates, she didn't do well one-on-one with men. After all that had happened, she would probably never date again. She had a couple of really great girlfriends to spend time with, but they were both married and busy with their own lives. And since she didn't go to church anymore, she didn't have much social interaction.

Yes, she would be alone the rest of her life.

Maybe Bert and Noreen would adopt her.

"So tell me about yourself," Jack said as they neared Tillamook.

Sophie hated that question. With a passion. But she was prepared to answer it. She had the answer memorized, and it was almost a reflex now.

"Not much to tell. I was born and raised in Southern Idaho. Graduated in communications from Boise State, got a job in Portland, and have lived there ever since."

"My mom's family is from a little town in Southern Idaho," he said.

She hated this part too. Everyone was always trying to make a connection, but no one ever did. Preston was just too small.

"She grew up in Preston."

Sophie felt her jaw drop.

"You know where Preston is?" he asked.

"Uh, yeah, actually, that's where I grew up."

"No kidding!" he exclaimed. "Small world. Did you know any Perrys? My mom was a Perry."

"I had a history teacher named Mr. Perry." She tried to remember his first name.

"Was he Nolan Perry?"

A bell went off in her head.

"Yes," she answered. "That's it. Nolan Perry. He got teacher of the year three years in a row. I really liked him."

"That's my mom's brother."

"How is he?" she asked. "He was one of my favorite teachers. I learned a lot from him because he made learning fun. He used to dress up like historical figures."

"He was like a father to me. During the summers he would bring his family and stay for a few weeks to help do repairs on our house and yard. He treated me like one of his own kids."

"You say *was;* did he pass away?"

"Last year. He died of colon cancer."

"I'm sad to hear that Mr. Perry died," she said softly. She hadn't thought of Mr. Perry for many years. Suddenly old feelings and memories were flooding her mind. She remembered how he made every student feel as though they were the most important person in the world to him.

"What about your family? Do they still live in Preston?"

There it was, the question she dreaded the most anytime she met someone new. The question she just couldn't answer. Especially this close to Christmas.

"Oh, I almost forgot!" she exclaimed, snatching her phone out of her purse. "I need to check my messages. Excuse me just a moment."

She checked her phone and actually found a new text message from her friend Amanda and one from

Ted at work. Amanda had offered her one last invitation to spend Christmas with her family, and Ted was letting her know that the project she'd assigned him before she left was completed and sitting on her desk. She knew she could count on Ted—that's why she'd given him the assignment. She was glad she'd put in for him to receive a nice Christmas bonus. He deserved it.

Caught up on her messages, she turned to Jack and tried another tactic to distract him from his previous interest in her background. "So, how do you think your mom is going to take this news?"

He shook his head. "She'll be surprised, but I think she'll be thrilled. She'll probably cry, but they'll be happy tears."

"She deserves that after all these years of wondering."

Jack slowed the car and pulled into a drive that led to a redbrick building with an large, elegant entryway. The place looked more like a five-star hotel than a care center.

"Gee, this is nice," Sophie remarked.

"It's the best in the area. They have a waiting list. A family friend owns the facility and helped get my mom in quickly. I wish she were happier here."

He pulled into a parking stall, then got out and met Sophie on the sidewalk. Sophie smiled nervously.

"Ready?" he asked, returning her smile.

She nodded.

"I think you two will like each other," Jack said as they walked to the entrance. "I wish you could've known my mother when she was younger. She was quite a woman." He held the door open for her as she stepped inside.

Inside, two giant staircases stretched up on either side of the foyer. Jack led her to the one on the right and protectively placed his hand at her back as they climbed the stairs, then guided her down a long hallway. They stopped at the room at the very end.

Sophie felt her heartbeat quicken. She felt awkward being present when such personal news was shared with a complete stranger.

"Should I wait out here until you tell her?"

He quickly shook his head. "She will want to know everything about how you found the bottle and got the note out. I want you there with me."

The way he said those last words made her feel like she belonged and was needed. She hadn't felt like that for a long time.

"It will be okay," he assured her. Then he took her by the hand and pushed open the door. "Mom?" he whispered as they walked in.

A woman lay in the bed, her slight frame barely detectable under the covers.

Jack pulled two chairs next to the bed and offered one to Sophie.

He took his mother's hand in his and patted it. "Mom." He tried to wake her, but she didn't stir.

Sophie didn't say anything, but she actually wondered if the woman were alive. Jack didn't seem worried, so she figured he was used to seeing his mother so out of it.

Sophie noticed a picture on the bedside table. She picked it up and saw that it was of Jack and an attractive woman dressed in stylish clothes. She had a nice smile—just like Jack's.

"She's very pretty."

"Thank you. She was quite beautiful in her day. She was little, but boy was she spunky. She took on the city council one time when she didn't agree with some ordinance they were trying to pass. She spoke her mind, and people respected her for it. She ran the lumberyard like a drill sergeant, I guess you could say. But her employees were loyal, and many of them stayed with her clear to the end. A lot of people in town encouraged her to run for mayor, but she didn't want to have anything to do with it."

"She sounds incredible," Sophie said, wishing she could be more in charge like that.

"Most people loved her. A few didn't like a woman as outspoken as she was. She can come across as a little blunt sometimes."

"I heard that," a weak voice said.

Jack looked at Sophie with raised eyebrows, like a little kid getting caught with his hand in the cookie jar.

"Hi, Mom," he said, lifting out of his chair and leaning over to give her a kiss on the cheek. "How are you today?"

"I'm fine, as long as I'm asleep. It's the part when I'm awake that I don't like. Did you remember to bring what I asked?"

"Yes, Mother."

"Well, can I have some?"

Jack looked at the door, his expression mischievous. Sophie wondered what was going on. "You know you're not supposed to have any."

"Oh, piddle!" his mother exclaimed. "I'm not going to spend my last few days on earth eating nothing but jello and clear broth!"

"Okay, okay," he said, shushing her. "Just a minute."

He got up and checked outside the door. When he came back, he pulled a small box out from inside his jacket.

Sophie smiled. Chocolate! She loved this woman already.

"Now don't eat the whole box all at once like you did last time," he lectured.

"Good grief, Jack, just give me a piece and quit treating me like a child."

The woman tried to sit up so she could accept the chocolate but needed some assistance.

Instinctively Sophie jumped up and helped prop another pillow under her shoulders.

Jack's mother recoiled and exclaimed, "Who in the Sam Hill are you?"

Sophie plopped back into her seat.

"She's a friend of mine, Mom. Her name is Sophie." He finished getting his mother situated and gave her a piece of chocolate.

"She can't have any of my chocolate," his mother said.

Sophie stifled a laugh. Jack cringed and mouthed, "Sorry," to Sophie. "Now, Mom. Be nice. Sophie came to share something very important with you."

"Oh?" she looked at Sophie suspiciously. "Is it good or bad?" She shoved the whole piece of chocolate into her mouth and eyed Sophie up and down, making Sophie feel very uncomfortable.

"It's good, Mom. You need to calm down and relax first before I let her tell you."

"I need another piece, then I'll be calm," his mother said.

"The nurses are going to hate me," he said as he took another chocolate out of the box. "This is the last one until after dinner."

He turned to Sophie and said quietly, "The nurses don't like her to eat it, because it gives her diarrhea."

Now it was Sophie's turn to cringe.

"What are you telling her?" his mother demanded. "I don't like it when you say things I can't hear."

Jack turned quickly to his mother. "I'm sorry, Mom. I forgot."

His answer appeased his mother, and she turned her interest to her chocolate.

After she finished the small, minty square and licked her fingers, she looked Sophie square in the eyes and said, "So, what's this big news?"

Sophie looked to Jack for help.

"Mom," he said, "Sophie has something wonderful to tell you, but you have to let her talk now. Okay?"

His mother let out a frustrated sigh. "Okay," she agreed, reclining back against the pillows. She gave Sophie a daring glare.

Sophie cleared her throat and said, "Well, you see, Mrs. McCrae—"

"Call me Viola," the woman ordered.

"Oh, okay, Viola. You see, I'm here visiting from Portland for the holidays—"

"You have family here?"

"No. No family here."

"Why aren't you with your family?"

"Mother," Jack said with measured patience. "If you wouldn't interrupt, she could finish her story. You can ask her questions later."

"Fine!" The woman pursed her lips together.

"Anyway, there was a big storm the night I arrived, and the day after I went for a walk on the beach, just a little south of Cannon Beach. While I was walking among the debris, I noticed a bottle wedged in with some seaweed. I picked up the bottle and noticed that there was a note inside."

Viola's expression turned from annoyed to mildly interested.

"I took the bottle back to the Cape House Bed-and-Breakfast, where I'm staying, and tried to open it, but the lid wouldn't budge. Bert, one of the owners of Cape House, helped me break it open so I could get to the note." Sophie stopped.

"I'm listening," Viola informed her.

"Well, the note was written to a woman named Viola and signed by someone named—"

"Ernest?" Viola whispered, her eyes wide open.

Sophie nodded.

"Mom," Jack leaned forward, "I think the note is from my father."

Viola placed her trembling hand over her open mouth.

Jack brought out the paper, still enclosed in its sheet protector. He held it close so she could see it.

Viola studied the handwriting, and tears filled her eyes. "Please," she said weakly, "read it."

Jack began:

*Dearest Viola,*

*The Devil's Wind is churning up the water something fierce. I know you may never get this message, but I have to write down how I feel.*

*How I wish I could hold you and tell you how sorry I am for the way we said good-bye. I would give anything to take back everything I said. Please, darling, forgive me. I love you. And I will love our child with all of my heart.*

*Tell your father that this is my last run. As soon as I get home, I'll go to work for him at Tillamook Lumber. I want to be home with you and our child, not gone for weeks at a time risking my life crab fishing.*

*I'll be home in time for Christmas, and we can talk then and plan our life together. Please forgive me.*

*I love you,*

*Ernest*

Viola shut her eyes. Her expression betrayed her emotions as tears leaked from the corners of her eyes.

Jack reached out and took his mother's hand.

"My dear Ernest," she said. "All these years." She cried softly while her son rubbed her hand. Then, when she had calmed some, she wiped at her wet face. Sophie handed her some tissue.

"In my heart I've always known he loved me and that he would have loved our son. When I found out the boat had capsized and that everyone on board had drowned, I still believed that my Ernest had found a way to survive and that some day he would return. We had our whole lives ahead of us."

She sniffled and dabbed at the tears on her cheeks some more.

"I'll never forget the first day we met." She had a faraway look in her eye, a smile playing on her lips. "I had graduated from college and was living in Portland, teaching high school English. I came home for summer break and was driving back from visiting a friend who'd just had a baby when I got a flat tire. I was fit to be tied! I didn't know what to do. Before I knew it a truck pulled up behind me and a handsome young man got out and walked up to my window and asked if I needed help. Of course I accepted his help, and he changed my tire and then proceeded to change my life."

Sophie noticed the peaceful expression on Viola's face as she talked about Ernest. She told how they'd started dating and how when it had come time for her to leave at the end of the summer, it was the hardest thing she'd ever done.

"Ernest told me that while I was at school he was going to work hard to save money so that the next summer when I came home we could be married. He had even decided to take a second job working as a commercial fisherman catching Dungeness crab. I didn't like it, because I knew how dangerous it was. But he was convinced that it was worth it so we could have enough money to get married. You see, my father didn't approve of Ernest. He didn't come from an affluent family, and he didn't have an education or career. But I knew Ernest was a good man, hardworking and kind. I loved him with all my heart."

Her eyes were filled with tears, but her mouth was getting dry from telling her story. Jack helped her get a sip of water, and she continued.

"The next summer when I returned, Ernest and I began to make plans to get married, but my father was still very much against it. My mother was too afraid of my father to defy him, but she loved Ernest also and was happy for me. She loved how well he treated me. Ernest vowed that he would prove to my father that he could be a good provider.

"Because of my father we put off the wedding until September, and then we decided we couldn't wait any longer. My father almost didn't attend the ceremony, but for the first time in her life my mother stood up to him. She told him that he was going to lose his only daughter if he didn't put his pride aside. So that's what he did. And after we got married, my father even offered Ernest a job at the lumberyard. But Ernest was also a proud man, and he wasn't about to take a handout from my father. He'd made good money during the previous winter catching crab, so, two months after we got married, he signed up again. When I found out I was very upset. I didn't want him to go, and I begged him not to. He got angry with me and said that he would prove to my father once and for all that he was good enough to marry his daughter. I'd never seen him so upset. We had a huge fight. We had decided to wait to start a family until we were able to build our savings and get financially secure, but I guess the Lord had other plans. I told Ernest that I was pregnant. I hoped that if he knew, he would change his mind. He nearly exploded."

She blew her nose, the emotion of nearly thirty years prior overwhelming her.

A nurse tapped on the door, interrupting the moment. Without pause she entered, carrying a tray of food for Viola.

"How are we today?" she said cheerfully, pulling a stand over next to the bed for the tray. "Are we hungry?"

The nurse obliviously went about getting the meal situated and raising Viola's bed so she could sit up higher. The woman told Viola about the weather outside and about the choir that would be coming later to sing Christmas carols.

After several minutes of arranging and incessant babbling, the nurse gave Viola one last smile and said, "Have a nice meal. I'll be back to check on you later."

"I can't wait," Viola said.

The room fell silent after the nurse left. Then Sophie and Jack looked at each other and started laughing. A smile broke across Viola's face and she joined in their laughter.

"I could have my head on backward and that nurse wouldn't notice," Viola said.

Sophie felt bad for Viola. She didn't doubt that Viola got adequate care, but she wondered if Viola felt like the workers really cared *about* her.

"Mom," Jack said, "you won't believe this, but Sophie is from Preston."

Viola looked up at Sophie and studied her. "Oh? Who's your family?"

Unable to avoid such a direct question, Sophie said, "My last name is Davis."

"Don't know any Davises. 'Course, I haven't been there for over thirty years. I bet it's changed a lot."

"Not too much," Sophie said, not admitting that she hadn't been back there in a long time either.

"My brother taught at the high school."

"He was my history teacher. Actually, he was my favorite teacher."

Viola smiled proudly.

"You should probably eat before your food gets cold," Sophie suggested.

"It won't matter," Viola said. "It doesn't taste any better hot!" She busied herself with checking out the meal that had been brought to her. Jack turned to Sophie and whispered, "I haven't heard her talk this much in months. She's never talked about how she met my father or what happened when he left that day."

"Jack!" Viola snapped. "What are you talking about?"

Once again Jack had been caught. "Sorry, Mom."

"Look at this slop!" Viola exclaimed. "What does a person have to do around here to get a decent meal?"

Jack stood and examined the food. Mashed potatoes, peas, some kind of meatloaf, red and green Jell-O cut up in squares, and a dinner roll that looked stale and dry.

He pulled a face.

"Now you see why I need the chocolate. It's the only thing that keeps me alive in here!" Viola confided to Sophie. "I would love some real food. Something with flavor and substance."

Sophie got an idea. She didn't have time to clear it with Bert and Noreen, but she had gotten to know them well enough to trust that they would go along with her.

"Jack," Sophie said. "Is Viola allowed to leave the facility?"

"Yes," he said. "I try to get her out as often as I can."

Sophie smiled and felt a fire of excitement ignite within her.

"Viola," Sophie said, "how would you like to go spend the night at the most charming bed-and-breakfast on the Oregon coast and have a wonderful Christmas meal tomorrow? Turkey, stuffing, candied yams."

"Will there be cranberries and pumpkin pie?" Viola asked.

"Yes. And homemade rolls and raspberry jam."

Viola's eyes went wide, then she looked at her son. "Jack, get me out of this place!"

Jack looked at Sophie. "Are you sure?"

"I'm positive. Noreen has crab cakes and clam chowder on the stove now and is making a delicious Christmas dinner for tomorrow, and she would love to have both of you there. And so would I," she added, looking him square in the eye.

The emotional connection between them grew at that moment. Sophie felt it, and somehow she knew Jack felt it, too.

"All the rooms but mine are empty at Cape House. Come and spend Christmas Eve with us. Unless you have other plans."

"Actually, I was just planning on spending the rest of the evening with my mother after I took you back."

"So you'll come?" Sophie asked, feeling her excitement grow.

"Mom," Jack said, "are you sure you feel up to it?"

"Just try and stop me," Viola said with a twinkle in her eye.

While Jack went to the office to make arrangements, Sophie stepped outside to make a phone call to Bert and Noreen. Just as she had expected, they were both thrilled that they would get to meet Viola and have more company for Christmas.

Sophie rushed back to Viola's room to share the news. Jack was still gone, and Viola was sitting on the edge of her bed, waiting for someone to help her get dressed.

"Noreen and Bert are anxious to meet you," Sophie told her.

"I'll be happy to see something besides these four walls. This is a thoughtful thing you are doing."

"Oh, it's nothing. I'm so happy it worked out. We'll take good care of you."

Viola reached for Sophie's hand. "I know you will. You have a good heart, my dear. I can see it in your eyes."

Sophie smiled.

"I also see pain and sadness. You have suffered much in your young life."

Sudden, unexpected tears stung Sophie's eyes. She turned her head, then got up from the bed and went to Viola's closet.

"Why don't I help you get dressed; then we can put a few things in an overnight bag," Sophie offered.

Viola didn't answer.

Sophie made sure her emotions were in check before turning back to Viola. "Would you like me to help you get ready?"

Viola looked up at her with eyes full of kindness and understanding. "Yes, dear, that would be nice."

The door to the room pushed open and Jack stepped inside.

"You're free to go, Mom. They were a little concerned about you going overnight, but I assumed full responsibility."

"They treat me like I'm a child!" Viola exclaimed. "I can fluff my own stinking pillows, you know!"

Jack and Sophie exchanged amused looks. The more Sophie was around Viola, the more she liked her.

*The Spirit of Christmas: Stories of the Season*

"Son, if you don't mind I'd like Sophie to help me get dressed. Why don't you go get my wheelchair, and we'll be ready when you get back."

Jack's eyebrows lifted in surprise. He looked at Sophie with questioning eyes.

"We'll be fine," she assured him.

"I'll be back in a few minutes then," Jack said, then left them alone.

Viola was right. She managed to get herself dressed with minimal assistance. They almost had her overnight bag packed when Jack returned.

He smiled at both of them. "I pulled the car up to the front," he said. "You two girls ready?"

Viola reached for Sophie's arm for support, and they were off for their holiday outing.

\* \* \*

Just as Sophie had expected, Bert and Noreen gave Viola a wonderful welcome to the inn. They had a chair ready for her near the fireplace, with a chenille throw and comfy footrest.

"I hope you plan on staying with us tonight," Noreen said. "We have a special room for you."

"This is so kind of you to take in a couple of strangers," Viola said.

"You don't feel like strangers to us," Noreen told her. "Now, before you get too comfortable, let's get you some dinner."

Jack wheeled his mother's chair to the dining room table.

"This place is incredible," Viola said as she was brought into the adjoining room. "So large and spacious, yet warm and inviting."

"It has a lot of charm," Noreen agreed.

They gathered around the table, fragrant with freshly baked rolls and homemade chowder and crab cakes.

Sophie noticed some color rising back into Viola's cheeks. The woman didn't even seem like the same person Sophie had met earlier that day.

The meal was delicious and satisfying, and even though she wasn't able to eat much, Viola couldn't stop raving about it. "Everything at the center is bland. I don't think they even know what spices are. I may have poor health, but I haven't lost my taste buds, for Pete's sake!"

Bert chuckled the loudest.

"Does anyone have room for dessert?" Noreen offered.

"I might have some room—depends on what you've got," Bert said, rubbing his ample belly.

"I've got a berry cobbler, a pecan pie, and several pumpkin pies."

"Did you say pumpkin pie?" Viola asked, her eyes lighting up with interest.

"I sure did."

"I have been craving pumpkin pie since Thanksgiving. We didn't have any at the center. Instead we got stewed apples with a little cinnamon." Viola pulled a face that proved amusing to the others. "That didn't work for me."

Everyone laughed.

"Well, none of that nonsense tonight," Noreen told her. "You get the real deal with plenty of whipped cream."

Viola clasped her hands together and beamed.

"You know," Bert said, "we have the perfect room for you, Viola. Noreen's mother stayed with us for about two years before she passed away. It's perfect for any of our guests who have special needs. I think you'll find it very comfortable."

Viola smiled, but her bottom lip began to tremble. She shut her eyes and dipped her head. Jack got to his feet and went to his mother, putting a comforting arm around her shoulder.

Using her napkin, Viola wiped her tears. "I'm sorry. It's just that this is all a little overwhelming. First the letter from Ernest and then being able to spend the holiday with you wonderful people. This is an answer to my prayers."

Jack leaned over and kissed his mother on the top of her head. "Mine too, Mom."

Sophie felt her own eyes well up as she watched the tender display of affection between mother and son. She was happy for the pair and grateful she was here with them.

\* \* \*

After they finished dessert, Sophie helped Noreen clean up the dishes. Then everyone gathered around the Christmas tree. An old upright piano stood next to it with a Nativity scene sprawled across the top.

Noreen sat down and offered to play Christmas carols. Viola was the first to make a request. "'Oh, Come, All Ye Faithful,'" she said. "I've loved that song since I was a little girl."

It had been three years since Sophie had even listened to, let alone sung, any Christmas carols. She hadn't been able to bear the pain attached to the whole Christmas season. But it was important to Viola, and she wanted to make sure the woman had a wonderful holiday.

Their voices started off soft, but by the end they were all singing their hearts out. Viola, touched by the song, kept a tissue close by to keep up with her tears.

Sophie noticed what a pleasant and rich voice Jack had. He shared a songbook with his mother, and she watched again how tenderly he cared for her, how attentive he was to her needs. She felt her heart, which had petrified over the past three years, begin to soften. Unexpected stirrings of emotion began to penetrate the hard exterior and get deep inside. Jack was handsome and kind and so easy to be around, something she wasn't used to with men. And Viola—well, she was just an amazing and special woman. Sophie knew that Viola saw through her, but it didn't make her feel uncomfortable. She liked that someone understood her pain.

After they sang a few songs around the brightly lit tree and cozy fire, Bert asked Jack if he would read the Christmas story.

With Bible in hand, Jack read the account of the Savior's birth.

Sophie listened intently, her thoughts focusing on the Savior's mission on earth, and for a moment, she understood the great love involved in His willingness to sacrifice His life for her. He alone knew of her pain and her heartache. He knew of her anger and confusion and lack of faith. She knew He loved her. And she loved Him, even though she hadn't allowed herself to feel it for a long while.

Tears began to flow. Sophie couldn't hold them back. They started as a leak but grew stronger.

Before the dam completely burst, Sophie got to her feet. "Excuse me," she whimpered, then bolted from the room. She flew up the stairs to the safety of her room, where she fell to her knees.

Draping her body over the bed, she began to sob. Three years of pain and heartache finally surfaced. Loss, confusion, anger, fear—all of those emotions and more flooded out of her. So much had been taken from her—everything important to her—but tonight she finally understood that so much had been given.

In that moment, in her deepest anguish, the healing began. The Balm of Gilead she'd read about in the scriptures was poured out upon her. Finally, after three years, she was ready to face her personal tragedy and move on.

\* \* \*

A light tap on Sophie's door broke the silence in her room. Her tears were gone, and she was exhausted.

"Yes?" she said.

"Sophie, it's Jack. Are you okay?"

Her tears had dried, but it would take much longer for her pillow to dry.

"Yes. I'm okay."

"Are you sure?"

"I'm sure."

"Do you want to talk?" he offered.

His invitation wasn't forceful or pushy but filled with concern and caring.

"Not now," she said. "Maybe another time, okay?"

"Okay. I guess I'll see you in the morning, then."

"Okay," she said. "Hey, Jack?"

"Yes?"

"Thank you."

"You're welcome, Sophie."

\* \* \*

Sophie woke up around midnight. She'd fallen asleep without even changing into her pajamas.

She got up and washed her face and brushed her teeth then changed her clothes.

Now that she was ready for bed, she was wide awake. And she was hungry.

A piece of Noreen's pumpkin pie sounded really good. She'd passed on dessert earlier, and now she was in the mood.

Without a sound she left her room, tiptoed down the hallway and stairs, and made her way to the kitchen. The house was quiet except for the tick of the clock on the mantel.

Turning on a small light over the kitchen sink, Sophie found a fork and a plate and cut a small triangle of pie.

At the table she took a bite of her pie and savored the spicy goodness as she reflected on the events of the past day that had impacted her life for the better. Viola was an inspiration and, in a way, felt like a kindred spirit. Meeting Viola had strengthened Sophie so she could confront her pain, allow it to surface and be released. And spending time with had Jack prompted, for the first time in a long time, stirrings in her heart. He was a wonderful guy, end of story. Handsome, devoted, charming, funny, intelligent . . . There was a warmth growing inside her, bubbling up as it expanded. Joy. She felt the wonderful sensation of joy. Happiness, peace, and hope, all rolled into one.

Tears stung her eyes with the realization, but this time they weren't tears of sorrow—they were tears of joy.

The next bite of pie was sheer heaven. She closed her eyes and licked her lips, enjoying the smooth, delicious mouthful.

"That pie must be pretty good," a voice said.

Sophie jumped and nearly choked as she swallowed.

"Jack!"

"I'm sorry, I didn't meant to startle you."

"I wasn't expecting anyone to be up," she said, wiping her mouth with a napkin.

"How is it?" he asked.

"Worth every calorie. I might have seconds."

"Mind if I join you?"

She smiled. "Not at all."

He got his own piece and joined her at the table. "Couldn't sleep?"

She cut a piece for him.

"I was asleep, but I woke up. I made the mistake of thinking about Noreen's pie. What about you? Why aren't you sleeping?"

"I had a lot on my mind."

"Oh? Anything you want to talk about?"

He took a bite of the pie. "Mmm, that is good." After he swallowed he answered her question.

"I think I made a mistake putting Mom in that care center. I felt like she was a whole new person tonight."

Sophie had noticed the transformation. "Doctors do the best they can, but they don't always factor in the human spirit."

"My mom has always had a purpose, something that got her up in the morning and gave her fulfillment. I don't think she has one foot in the grave like the doctors have told me. She just needs something to live for!"

"I think you're right. Did you see how she came alive when she found out she was spending Christmas here? With other people and real food?"

Jack sliced another bite with his fork, then paused in contemplation. He looked at Sophie and said, "I'm getting her out of there!"

Sophie gave him an approving smile. "That's great. She's not ready for that place yet."

"They aren't ready for her either!" he said.

They both laughed.

"Now," Jack's expression grew serious again, "how are you?"

"You know what?" she answered with enthusiasm. "I'm doing great."

His brows lifted in surprise. "Really? Because you . . ."

"Fell apart last night?"

"I wouldn't exactly say that."

"I would," she responded. "I finally realized some things last night, and they all kind of overwhelmed me."

"What kinds of things?"

She looked at him, realizing that this was a question that had once had the power to freeze her.

Not anymore.

"Three years ago, on Christmas Eve, my parents and my brother were driving to Portland to be with me for Christmas, and they were caught in a horrible snowstorm. My mom had just talked to me on her cell phone and had told me that the roads were getting really bad. I told them to turn around and that I would try to get a flight the next day to come see them, but they were more than halfway there, and they were determined to come. They assured me they would be fine and that if it got worse they'd pull over and get a room for the night.

"A few hours later I got another call. They were in a terrible accident." She choked up and could barely talk. "My mother and brother were killed immediately . . ." She fought to keep control. "My father was airlifted to the hospital in Boise. He died on the way there."

Her voice cracked with emotion again, but she was able to continue.

"It's been so hard, especially at the holidays. I try to get away, go somewhere to get my mind off the memories."

"That's why you're here, alone, on Christmas," he said.

"You were wondering?" she asked.

"Yes. I felt bad you were away from your family for the holidays."

"Friends, even coworkers, invited me to spend the holidays with them, but I didn't want to celebrate. I didn't even want to remember it was Christmas."

"I can see why," Jack said. "I guess that means you don't have a boyfriend?"

Sophie couldn't stop the smile that broke onto her face. He *was* interested!

"No. Not anymore. I was engaged at the time of the accident. My fiancé stayed with me through the initial shock of it all, and the funerals. But as weeks turned to months, I couldn't snap out of the depression. He couldn't take it any longer, and he broke off our engagement."

"I'm sorry."

Sophie shrugged. "It turned out to be a blessing in disguise. He wasn't right for me. But at the time I just felt very alone. I've felt that way ever since. Until now."

"Oh? What happened to change it?"

"Being here, finding that message, meeting your mother, and . . . you."

Now it was his turn to smile.

"You're the first man I've been around that I've been comfortable with," she told him. "I've really appreciated it."

"I've felt that way too," he said.

"Something happened last night, when you were reading out of the Bible. Those words have never meant so much to me. But when I heard you read them," she swallowed, "I don't know how to explain it. I felt them, deep down. I understood the Savior's mission and what it actually meant for me personally."

She clutched at her heart as tears filled her eyes. "Jack," she smiled through her tears, "I finally feel peace inside."

He smiled back at her and reached for her hand, which she gave freely.

"I lost faith in the Lord. I didn't trust Him, because He let this happen. But listening to the story of His birth, I felt His love for me. I knew without a doubt He loved me. And that I could trust Him.

"He took my pain. It's a miracle. He has taken my burden, just like He said He would. I just had to give it to Him."

Jack blinked as his own eyes misted over. "It is a miracle. Just like finding that message in the bottle was a miracle."

"Right!" she said. "I know that God guided me here. This week has changed my life."

"And mine too," he said.

Their eyes locked and, wordlessly, they were drawn into each other's arms.

Wrapped in the strength he offered, Sophie shut her eyes and offered a prayer of thanks. Her heart was nearly bursting with gratitude. She had never felt more loved by her Savior than at that very moment— a moment she would never forget.

\* \* \*

"Merry Christmas," Sophie nearly sang as she bounded down the stairs the next morning.

The first person she saw was Viola, sitting in her wheelchair next to the Christmas tree.

"Don't you look radiant this morning!" Viola exclaimed.

"Do I?" Sophie said with a laugh. "I feel radiant." She gave the woman a gentle hug. "And you look absolutely beautiful," Sophie told her.

"Noreen came in early and helped me get ready. She did my hair, and did you notice? She even put a little makeup on me. I haven't worn lipstick in months!"

"I did notice. You look twenty years younger."

"I feel it!" Viola exclaimed.

"My goodness!" Noreen said, coming into the room, "What's all the excitement about?"

Sophie rushed to Noreen and gave her a hug. "Merry Christmas, Noreen."

"Thank you, dear. Merry Christmas to you."

"Let me help you in the kitchen. You deserve the day off."

"Oh, fiddlesticks. I'm fine."

"Please, let me help. I can peel potatoes or something," Sophie pleaded. Then she turned to Viola. "And you can join us."

"I would like that very much!" Viola exclaimed.

The women moved their excitement into the kitchen, where Noreen was creating a masterpiece for Christmas dinner.

Sophie went to work peeling potatoes, and Viola began folding napkins and giving the silver a final polish so the table would look just right.

The women chatted as they worked in anticipation of a wonderful meal with loved ones and friends.

"Well, for Pete's sake," Bert exclaimed as he banged in the back door. "Noreen, I've never see you put our guests to work before."

The women laughed.

"We had to beg her," Sophie said. "And by the way," she went to Bert and gave him a hug, "merry Christmas."

Bert chucked. "Well, merry Christmas to all of you. It sure smells good in here."

"I've got some muffins and juice if you're hungry," Noreen said. "I'm not fussing for breakfast since we're going to stuff ourselves in a few hours."

"I'll come get a bite in a minute. I've got a piece of fence out there that blew over in the storm the other night that I want to fix."

"Could you use some help?"

They all turned to see Jack enter the room. Sophie's heart fluttered at the sight of him. Immediately, his eyes met hers, and he gave her a small smile.

Jack didn't even wait for Bert's reply. He walked straight to Sophie and pulled her into a hug. "Merry Christmas," he said.

With a potato in one hand and a peeler in the other, she returned his hug. "Merry Christmas to you, Jack."

When they stepped apart, they were met by the surprised expressions of Noreen and Bert. Viola, however, looked quite pleased.

"Did I miss something?" Bert asked.

"Apparently so," Noreen said, "But isn't it wonderful!"

"I had a feeling about you two," Viola said. She pointed at Sophie with the fork she'd been polishing. "You're an answer to my prayers."

Sophie went to Viola and knelt down beside her. "And you are an answer to mine." She gave Viola another hug, then stood up. "All of you have been." More tears threatened, but she quickly blinked them away. No more tears, she decided. It was time for joy.

Jack smiled at her again as he followed Bert out the door.

For the first time in a long time, Sophie felt complete as she thought of her miraculous vacation. She would never have to dread Christmas again. Now she had new, wonderful memories to replace the tragedy and loss the holidays had come to mean to her. She knew that this was just the beginning of something wonderful. Something lasting.

She had lost her family, but she had found a new one to help celebrate the first of many wonderful Christmases to come.

# About the Authors

*Jennie Hansen*

Jennie Hansen graduated from Ricks College in Idaho, then Westminster College in Utah. She has been a newspaper reporter, editor, and librarian. In addition to writing novels, she reviews LDS fiction in a monthly column for Meridian Magazine.

She was born in Idaho Falls, Idaho, and has lived in Idaho, Montana, and Utah. She has received numerous writing awards.

Jennie and her husband, Boyd, live in Salt Lake County. They have five married children and ten grandchildren.

Jennie enjoys hearing from her readers, who can visit her website, www.jennielhansen.com, or who can write to her in care of Covenant Communications, P.O. Box 416, American Fork, UT 84003-0416, or via e-mail at info@covenant-lds.com.

*Betsy Brannon Green*

Betsy Brannon Green currently lives in Bessemer, Alabama, which is a suburb of Birmingham. She has been married to her husband, Butch, for twenty-nine years, and they have eight children, one daughter-in-law, two sons-in-law, and three grandchildren. She loves to read—when she can find the time—and watch sporting events, if they involve her children. She is a Primary teacher and family history center volunteer in the Bessemer Ward. She also works in the office at the Birmingham Temple. Although born in Salt Lake City, Betsy has spent most of her life in the South. Her writing and her life have been strongly influenced by the town of Headland, Alabama, and the many generous and gracious people who live there. Her first book, *Hearts in Hiding*, was published in 2001, followed by *Never Look Back* (2002), *Until Proven Guilty* (2002), *Don't Close Your Eyes* (2003), *Above Suspicion* (2003), *Foul Play* (2004), *Silenced* (2004), *Copycat* (2005), *Poison* (2005), *Double Cross* (2006), *Christmas in Haggerty* (2006), *Backtrack* (2007), *Hazardous Duty* (2007), and *Above and Beyond* (2008).

*Michele Ashman Bell*

Michele grew up in St. George, Utah, where she met her husband at Dixie College before they both served missions, his to Pennsylvania and hers to Germany and California. Seven months after they returned, they were married and are now the proud parents of four children: Weston, Kendyl, Andrea, and Rachel.

Michele is the best-selling author of several books and a Christmas booklet and has also written children's stories for the *Friend* magazine.